Sha.

Sins and Scars

Draconic Crimson MC

Book 1, The Sinners Series

K. Renee

K. Renee

K. Renee

Content

Copyright

Sins and Scars

© 2016 K. Renee

Published by K. Renee

1st Edition

author's work.

Published: K. Renee - 2016

k.renee.author@gmail.com

Cover Design: KLa Boutique - Swag

https://www.facebook.com/pages/KLa-Boutique-Swag/908193265872628

Formatting: K. Renee

Cover Photo: © Wander Aguiar

https://www.facebook.com/Wander-Book-Club-461833027360302

Cover Model: David Byers

Editor: TCB Editing Services

https://www.facebook.com/TCBEditing/?fref=ts

ISBN-13: 978-1533107367

ISBN-10: 153310736X

Every saint has a past, and every sinner has a future

— Oscar Wilde

K. Renee

chapter One

One year. Six months. Five days. Three hours.

That's how fuckin' long it's been since I last saw my girl. She told me it was over, but she doesn't know that I won't fuckin' let her leave me without a fight. I gave her time, but now, I'm claiming her. She doesn't get that me and her are in this shit together. We fuckin' belong together, and there is no other bitch I want by my side.

Strutting into the clubhouse, I see her short skirt and four-inch stilettos before I even see the rest of her sexy-as-fuck body. I sent my Sergeant at Arms to bring her ass back, and I already know the hellcat is going to come in claws out, waiting to fucking strike.

My eyes roam up her body and I can't help but groan when I get to her perfect tits. She has a body of a porn star, and sure knows how to fucking use it to her advantage. She wasn't always the spitfire she is now. When I first met her, she was as shy as a baby bird.

Her eyes meet mine, and I can see the hatred in them. I wait for her to reach me before I even say a word to her. She knew I wasn't giving her up. I told her when she left that I would never let someone else have her. She's been mine since she turned eighteen, and that isn't ever going to fuckin' change.

"How fucking dare you!" She screams at me. Before I can stop her, she slaps me. Her face is turning red and I can see the anger seeping through her pores. She didn't believe me. My Vice President goes towards her, but I hold my hand up stopping him.

"She-" He stops when I give him a look. I don't give a shit what she does at this moment as long as she is standing here in my clubhouse.

Walking closer to her, I wrap a dark strand of her hair around my finger. She tries to bat my hand away, but I don't release her hair. She winces when I tug on it, but when she looks up at me, I see a different look in her eyes.

"Stav." She growls.

She goes to slap me again, but this time I'm ready for her. I grab her wrist and put it behind her back, pulling her body to mine. I press my erection against her to let her know just how much I love when she fights me. I love that she isn't a fuckin' push over like most of the bitches around here. She gives it to me just as hard as I give it to her.

"Harlyn." Her name rolls off my tongue and she looks like I burned her just by saying her name.

"Don't touch me." She spits. I grab her arm and she tries to pull out of my grip, but she's not strong enough.

"You sent one of your fucking lunatic best friends to come and get me. What the fuck is wrong with you?" She pushes against my chest, but she isn't going anywhere.

"What baby, you don't like Dex?" I grin down at her, and when I look over her shoulder, I see a smirk on his face. My orders to him were to bring her home. I didn't give a fuck what he had to do to get her here, just that she needed to be here.

"No!" She says with a disgusted look. What she doesn't know is that I've had a man on her this whole time. I heard reports of what she's done in the time we've been apart, and I will make sure she forgets every fucking bastard she ever let inside of her.

"That bastard killed him." She tries to go after him, but I wrap my arm around her waist to stop her.

"Who?" I grip her chin and force her to look at me.

"My boyfriend." She whispers. I see her eyes start to fill with tears, and I pull her towards my office. Typically I don't give a fuck if bitches are crying in front of my men, but Harlyn is mine, and I'll be damned if anything upsets her. When I get her through the door, I close it behind us and push her up against it.

"Boyfriend?" I whisper in her ear. She nods her head and doesn't say anything else.

"Did he fuck you the way I do?" I feel her body shiver and I know that I still affect her the same way I did when I had her. She doesn't like to admit it, but I'm the only one who has ever fucked her the way she really likes it. Harlyn likes it rough. She likes it when I spank her ass, and tie her to the bed. She doesn't like that sweet and loving bullshit like she wants them to believe.

"He was nothing like you. You're a fucking monster." Her voice is barely above a whisper.

"If I was such a damn monster, than why the fuck am I making you wet right now?" Her eyes snap to mine and she tries to push me away again. I shove my hand down the front of her skirt and I feel her wetness through her lace panties.

"Don't fucking touch me." She snaps, pulling away from me. I let her go this time, but I don't move from where I'm standing at the door. She isn't escaping so soon. I will lock her ass in my fucking room if I have to.

"You can be mad all you fucking want baby, but I already told you that you're mine and there is no fucking way I'll let you keep making me look like a damn fool." She looks over her shoulder at me and this time she has a different look on her face.

"Really? I'm yours? Are you fucking kidding me, Stav? You lost all right to call me yours when I found you with your dick in some other whore's mouth." Shaking my head at her, I can't help but think that maybe she is fucking crazy. I never once had my dick in some other bitch's mouth while she was mine.

Stalking towards her, I back her up against the desk and cage her in. "You know damn well that I never stuck my dick in another bitch while I had your fuckin' ass in my bed. Stop bringin' up shit that happened before I had you. You weren't even fucking legal when you saw me with that bitch. Not once since you turned eighteen did I fuck someone other than you."

"You trying to say you didn't fuck anyone this whole time I've been gone?" Her eyes are narrow, and she looks ready to slit my throat with my own knife. Her hands go to my chest and I know she's already looking for it. Little does she know, I already knew what her next move would be. I moved the normal place for my knife, just in case she'd try.

"You left me. I had to lick my wounds somehow.

I know for sure that you've been whoring your damn way through Vegas." She slaps me again, and I bend her over the desk and slide my hand up her skirt. She tries to fight me for a minute, but the second my fingers sink into her, all her attempts at getting away fall away, and she pulls my head down, kissing me like she's starved for me.

I don't even bother trying to figure out her right now. I just give her what we're both craving. Pushing her skirt up around her waist, I slide her panties to the side and move my hand to my jeans to unbuckle my belt, unbuttoning them in the same move. Sliding them down enough to get my dick out, I don't even think twice about slamming into her pussy. She says she doesn't like me because I'm a monster, but I already know that it's so far from the damn truth.

She's always had a soft spot for me, even when she saw the side of me that only she could calm.

I fuck her hard and fast, causing the desk to move a couple inches every few thrusts. Her hands grip the back of my neck, and she pulls me down for another scorching hot kiss. Her dark hair fans out over my desk, and I wrap my fingers around her neck as I thrust my hips into her. Her moans fill the room, and I can't get enough of her body. My hand slides up her body and I cup one of her perfect tits through her tight shirt.

She pulls my head down and I let her claim my

mouth. Her tongue slips between my lips and I can feel her tightening around me. "Stav." She moans louder this time.

Running my lips down her neck, I see the burn from my beard hair on her skin. She's going to be fucking pissed when she sees the marks, but I don't give a fuck. She's mine, and I'm going to make sure every motherfucker out there knows it.

My balls start to tighten, and her nails dig into my forearm. "Come for me baby. Give me what we both want so fuckin' bad right now." She raises her hand to hit me again, but I put it above her head, and pull out of her completely.

"Stavros." She growls.

I pull away from her and she gives me a scathing look.

"What do you want Harlyn?" Her lips turn into a frown and she fixes her skirt.

"I want you to leave me the fuck alone. We've been done for over a year, and now you're just fucking ruining my life."

Grabbing her around the waist, I pull her body to mine and she gets weak in the knees. "You and I both know that isn't true. I fucking love you, and would do anything to protect you. You think that pussy Dex put a bullet in would have killed for you? You think that pussy

15

would fuck you the way you begged me to? You think that that pussy knows every fuckin' thing about you? No. He doesn't fuckin' know shit. He would have never made you happy, baby girl. I'm the only man that will fucking die for you."

She pushes at my chest, and I pick her up and set her on my desk. Her skirt goes around her hips again and I could easily slam right back into her if I wanted to. Tilting her hips, I slide back into her, and her head falls back as her mouth slowly opens into an O shape.

I pound into her roughly until we both come. As her pussy tightens on my dick, I feel like I'm coming home. "Oh God, Stav!" She screams. She milks my cock as I thrust into her until we both come down from our orgasms.

Dropping my body onto her, I kiss her neck and suck on her pulse hard enough to leave a mark. She doesn't even bother to try and stop me. I'm sure she already knows why I'm doing it. I won't let any of my men touch her, and I sure as hell ain't letting my girl leave again.

Her fingers tangle in my hair and she gives it a good yank. The pain gets me hard again, and I'm pretty sure she wasn't expecting that. "I hate you Stavros. I hate you for bringing me back here when you promised me that I was free. You had your sergeant kill my boyfriend, and drag me back here kicking and screaming. Do you even care what he did?"

Looking down at her face, I see the tears starting to pool in her eyes, and I don't feel even a bit of guilt. I've done everything in order to protect her, but having her away from me isn't the fuckin' answer anymore. I'm done letting her run around on me. I get she's still pissed at me for who the fuck knows what anymore, but it's time for her to come home for good.

"Did he hurt you?" I don't get completely off of her, but I pull back enough to read her face. At first, she looks like she is going to say that he did, but she shakes her head no. If he had laid a hand on her in any other way than making sure her ass got to the clubhouse, I would castrate him before burying my knife into his throat.

"He didn't touch me; if that's really all you want to know." She turns her head to the side and looks at the door. She wants to run, but I won't let her.

"You love him?" my voice is low and I can see the way her eyes widen at my question.

"Yes." She bites out. Just by the tone of her voice, I know that she is fucking lying to me. I grab her chin in my hand, and force her to look at me. When our eyes meet, I can see all the emotions laid out right before me. She's never been all that good at keeping shit from me. It's one of the reasons I let her stay away for a little while longer than I originally planned. She's lucky I didn't have my man put a bullet in every fucker's head that even touched her - shit, even if they looked at her..

Slowly pulling out of her, I run my hand down her neck and stop on her tit. Rubbing my thumb over her nipple, I see the lust in her eyes. "Don't lie to me Harlyn. I know you didn't love him." She frowns and pushes me up and off of her.

"I won't lie to you. I already know that you feed on that shit." She adjusts her skirt and panties before she sits on the desk.

"The only thing I feed into is pissing you the fuck off." She shakes her head at me and I grin.

"I don't know why you just don't make this easier on yourself." She turns her head away from me, and I continue. "Harlyn, you and I both know that you've been mine since before you were eighteen. I waited to claim you for a reason. I knew that you would hate this life, and the man I became, but you're it for me, and I will fight like fuckin' hell to keep you in this life with me. You are the only thing I live for anymore."

Her eyes widen and she shakes her head at me. She goes to say something, but she can't get the words out. "Cat got your tongue baby girl?" I run my fingers down her jaw and she frowns.

"I love you Har, and I will do everything to make sure you're safe and loved. But I need you to trust me.

For once, don't give me your shit. I don't mind your feisty little attitude behind closed doors, but you need to stop running your damn mouth in front of my men. I am still the man you fell in love with."

"No you're not!" She screams at me. "You don't know how bad you hurt me! I fucking trusted you! I loved you, and look at what that got me." She points to herself and I don't get what she's trying to tell me. "I'm a fucking mess! I can't even fall in love with a normal man because you've fucking ruined me!"

"Harlyn." I state, but before I can continue, she stops me.

"Don't fucking Harlyn, me!" she gets off my desk and starts to move towards the door, but I stop her before she can leave.

"Do not leave this clubhouse, or I will lock you in my room. You're free to roam the building, but do not disobey me, Harlyn, or I will hunt you down." Her eyes widen and she looks a little pale. She doesn't say anything to that, but I can tell that she might actually listen to me this time.

Chapter Two

I let her lead me back into the bar area of the clubhouse because I'm sure she needs to cool down. Shit, so do I. I want so bad to bend her over my desk and spank her tight little ass for the disrespect she showed me when she first walked in the clubhouse, but I didn't.

If my men talked to me the way she did, I would have their heads. They all know I'm a sucker for the girl, and there isn't one person that would think to say anything except Romeo, my VP. When I see him, he motions for me to come towards him.

I wrap my arm around her waist before she gets too far away from me. "Behave." She turns and gives me the stink eye before turning back towards the bar. Before I release her, I give her one more piece of advice. "Any of my men touch you because you can't keep yourself from proving a damn point to me; their blood is on your hands." I feel her body tense up, and when she turns around she looks even angrier than before.

"You don't own me Stav. I can fuck, and flirt with whomever I damn well please." Her voice isn't more than a whispered yell. She thinks that I won't kill anyone who touches her? She has another thing coming.

"I do own you. Mind, body, and soul, babe. You just seem to forget. Give me a kiss." She pushes my chest, and I give her ass a squeeze.

"You're a pig." She breathes. I can feel her body start to react to me and I know she wants me as bad as I want her. Fucking other bitches never gave me the satisfaction that she just gave me in my office. Her body has always been made for mine, and the quicker she realizes that, the easier this shit can go. We have enemies that are ready to declare full blown war on us, and the only thing I can care about is making sure she's safe.

"Kiss." I growl this time. She searches my face for a second before she pinches my nipple and walks towards the bar. Shaking my head, I can't help but grin. She's feistier now more than ever before, and I can only imagine what the sex is going to be like when she finally submits to me again.

I watch her ass sway from side to side as she walks to the bar and orders a drink from one of the new prospects. He almost looks scared of her. I can only guess the look she's giving him right now. She can be a real bitch when she wants to, and I know all her anger is aimed right at me. Mick just happens to be the poor bastard in front of her to take her wrath.

Making my way over to Romeo, I see him watching her, too. He's never really been a fan of her since she up and left, but I don't give a fuck. She's mine, and there is nothing that will ever change that.

"You got any news for me?" I ask taking a seat on the barstool next to him.

"Just that you got to her before they did. She was in the wind. I'm actually surprised you found her." I smirk at that. Mick brings us both beers and I take a healthy swig of mine before setting it on the bar behind me.

"She was never in the wind. I had an old friend keep a close eye on her. Nothing would have happened to her. He would have killed them all before they touched her." He looks at me for a second and shakes his head.

"Prez, you know I've got nothing but fucking respect for you, but is she really worth the fucking headache? I mean she's fucking hot and all, but the bitch is fucking crazy. She slapped you in front of your men, and you didn't do shit to her." He stares at me waiting my reply. I don't owe any of these fuckers any explanation, but since he's my VP, and one of my closest friends, I give it to him.

"I love her. I've loved her since before she was eighteen, and I won't stop fucking loving her. Trust me, I tried to get over her when she left, but that bitch is buried so far down deep inside me, that I can't find where she ends and I begin. She acts like she couldn't give a fuck about me, but the minute I put my hands and mouth on her, she can't get me to fuck her fast enough."

He shakes his head and looks over at her again, which causes me to look at her. She's bending over the bar, and has her tits pressed up to her chin while she talks to Mick. A few of the guys behind her are now staring at her ass and panties that are probably on display. "I'll be back." I grit out.

Getting off the barstool, I make my way towards her. When I get close to her, my men all look away. Grabbing the ends of her hair, I pull her head back, and she glares at me. "I'm not your little whore that you can fuck whenever the urge arises. I already told you that you don't own me, so I will do what I want, when I want, for as long as you keep me prisoner here." I pull her back into my chest, and whisper in her ear.

"You sure you want to go down this route? I'm done being fucking nice to you. You want to act like a whore? Go for it. I will cut off any one of my men's dicks, and feed it to them if they so much as touch one hair on your beautiful head." She stiffens in my arms, and I wait for her to say something else to piss me off.

"You wouldn't kill one of your own men just because I let them touch me." She challenges. I release her hair and she moves back into a sitting position on the barstool.

Turning to the room, I eye each and every one of my men before telling them what I'll do if any of them think of touching her. "For those of you fuckers that don't know, this here is Harlyn, and she's my ol' lady. Any of you fuckers touch her, and I'll cut your dicks off and feed them to you. I don't give a fuck what she tells you, she's mine." All my men grunt out their understanding, and when I look back at her, she's fuming. The pissed off expression does nothing but turn me on, and she knows it. Sometimes I think she does this shit just to get a reaction out of me.

She storms off, and I follow behind her. She makes her way towards my room and flings the door open, letting it hit the wall with a thud. Pulling the door closed with me, I make my way towards her. She flops down on the bed and I lay down next to her. When she turns her face towards mine, I see it. I see the bottled up hurt and anger written all over her face.

"Why won't you just let me live my life like I've been doing for the last year and a half? I was happy,

Stav. I was finally moving on." Staring into her eyes, I try to find the truth in them. She wasn't happy. She's just pissed that I'm not giving her an option anymore.

"You really want some pussy son of a bitch to protect you, baby?" She doesn't say anything, just glares at me.

"You want the truth?" I ask. She turns on her side and looks at me, waiting for me to give her the truth. She isn't going to like it, but there is nothing I can do about that. This is more than just us now. I'm protecting her and my brothers from the shit storm that is about to come our way.

"Yes Stav. I just want you to tell me the truth like you used to." Reaching out, I run my fingers over the side of her face. She closes her eyes and sucks in a breath. I still affect her, just like she affects me.

"The Fighting Rebels want you. Their president threatened to kill you." Her eyes widen and she scoots a little closer to me. "That's the reason I sent Dex to get you. They have a bounty on your pretty little head, and they won't stop until they get their hands on you. I won't let them take the only good fuckin' thing I've ever had. I know I've fucked us up, but babe I will do everything in my power to protect you. I need you to trust that I will keep you safe."

Tears start to pool in her eyes, and she tries to blink them away. Wrapping a hand around the back of her neck, I pull her body into mine. She buries her face into my chest and I can only think about the shit we've been through over the last few years. When I first met her, she wasn't the feisty, take no-shit-from-me, woman. She was quiet and collected. She didn't know that I would come into her life and turn it upside down.

Kissing the top of her head, I hold her until she stops crying. "Why do they want me?" She finally asks. Sighing, I rub my hand down her back trying to think of a good way to say this shit.

"Because of me." She pulls away from me, but she doesn't get too far. Using my body weight, I push her into the mattress so she can't run away this time. She wanted the truth, and I'm going to give it to her, no matter how much it hurts her.

"The wrong person found out about you, and I tried to fix this shit to give you what you wanted, but there is nothing I can do now but bring you back under my protection."

"Why do they care about me? What would finding me do to help them?" She's angry, and I get that. I'll let her be angry all she wants, but she isn't leaving here. She can bitch and moan for months, and it still won't do shit.

"Because they know that they can hurt me by going after you. The Fighting Rebels want something from me, and the only way I'll ever give it up is if your life was on the line." She gasps and tries to pull back, but I don't let her.

"What do you have of theirs?" Her eyes search mine, looking for an answer, but I rather not tell her stuff that doesn't concern her.

"It's better you don't know. If they somehow get you, you won't be able to give them what they want." She swallows, and I watch the way her throat moves.

"Stavros, I swear to God, if you don't tell me, then I'm walking out this door, and never coming back. Stop fucking lying to me. I deserve to know the damn truth when it's me they want."

"You only need to know what I want you to know, babe. I make the fucking rules here, and you will abide by them." She huffs out and gets off the bed. I let her go because I know that if I don't, all we are going to do is end up in a fuckin' screaming match, and that won't solve a damn thing. All she fuckin' needs to know is that I am the one protecting her, and making sure that nothing happens to her. She doesn't deserve the life I've brought her in, but there ain't no way in hell that I'll let her go now. She's been the air I've breathed since I first saw those pouty little lips and bangin' fucking body at the clubhouse.

She scurries into the bathroom in my room, and slams the door shut.

A knock at the door sounds and I pull myself off

the bed to answer it. I see Blitz, and he has a frown on his face. "Yeah?" I watch him as he tries to figure out a way to say whatever the fuck it is. He doesn't talk much as it is, but he's deadly as fuck.

"Delilah is here." I mentally groan at his words. Just fucking great. This is all I need. That bitch has been trying to get me to wife her up for the last year, when I want no part of her whore ass. I made the mistake in fucking her a few times, and apparently, she thought that it meant I was handing my balls over to her, too.

"I'll deal with her in a minute." I grumble. He turns and makes his way down the hall. Hearing Harlyn clear her throat, I turn my head and close the door behind me.

"Real classy Stavros, you've been fucking the biggest whore in the whole damn place. Let me guess, she claimed you as hers?" I can see the sneer on her face and it lets me know that she's jealous. She doesn't want to admit it, but she is still mine.

"Jealous babe?" She snorts at that and I raise an eyebrow at her.

"I couldn't be jealous of a whore that is so desperate she has to make up stories in her head just to make herself feel better when she sucks your cock." Her nose wrinkles at her own words and I know she doesn't mean it. She's jealous, and I can't wait to see what she does.

Chapter Three

Making my way out of the room and into the bar, I scan the area for Delilah, and come up empty. I turn around and see Harlyn staring at me. "Disappointed?" She has a grin on her face and I close the distance between us, wrapping my arms around her waist

"No. I already have my ol' lady in my arms. What more could I possibly want?" Her fuckin' stripper heels put her at just the right height. Before I can say or do anything else, I hear that bitch Delilah screaming at me. Harlyn's lips curve into a grin and I know she loves this. She loves seeing me annoyed as fuck.

"Stavros!" her voice carries across the room and when I release Harlyn and turn around, I can see that shit's about to get crazy in here. She goes right towards Harlyn and I step in front of my girl. "Keep your hands off the trash. You are way above her whore ass."

Before I can even stop her, Harlyn moves in front of me.

"Whore ass? Are you shitting me? At least I don't get fucked by every one of his brothers and then come begging to suck his dick. I have way more class than that, bitch." Delilah comes closer and I try and step between her and Harlyn again. I motion to Dex, and he grabs Delilah around the waist and hauls her backwards a few feet.

"Stavros, you and I have something." She whines. I don't do bitches trying to claim me when they aren't even a damn blip on my radar. The only woman I'll ever let claim my dick is the one I now have a hand on. My hand is on her stomach and I'm keeping her against me.

"We don't have shit. I told you that from day one, and I would never make you into my ol' lady. I've had one for years and that shit ain't changing." Harlyn turns and glares at me, but I don't give a fuck. She will give into me again. I don't have any doubts.

"I'm not your ol' lady!" Harlyn yells at me. I shake my head and look over her head at Delilah who is now about to blow a damn gasket.

"Get her out of here. If she can't handle being around my ol' lady, then she's gone." Dex nods his head before leading a kicking and screaming Delilah who is now throwing out insults at my girl left and right.

Looking back down at Harlyn, I can see that it doesn't even faze her.

When the doors shut, the room falls silent and the only thing I can see is her. "Your sins follow you everywhere, Stav. They've left scars on me, on you, and everyone around you. I don't know how you can live with yourself." She pulls out of my arms and she rushes back down the hallway towards my room.

I don't stop her, and I don't follow her this time. She's going to find out that this shit isn't over, even if I have to tie her to the bed so I can tell her what she wants to know. Thinking back to the day I met her, I can't help but grin. She was so damn pure and innocent.

Four Years Ago

Walking into the clubhouse, I see that my brothers are throwing another party. People are fucking everywhere and I scan the room. Girls are practically running around naked, and a few of my brothers are trying to bag one of them for the night. We party hard, and we fuck harder. That's something we've always prided ourselves on. Not to mention all the shit we do during the day. Last week, I stuck a knife in the throat of a man who tried to steal our shipment from us. I didn't even think twice about what I was doing. The only thing I cared about was making sure the bastard who crossed us paid for his sins.

Walking over to the bar, I see a new face and I can't help but check her out. She's wearing a short, cutoff skirt, and a tight tank top that pushes her tits up. She's talking to Trixie, one of the club whores that has been with us a few years. She doesn't look like the type to be messed up in an MC, but I sure am glad she's here.

Romeo comes up to me and slaps me on the shoulder. "Fuck man, where did Trixie find that hot little bitch?" I shrug my shoulder, but don't take my eyes off of her. She has fuckin' legs for days that would look sexier if they were wrapped around my neck as I ate her pussy for breakfast, lunch, and dinner.

"You've got that look." He grins. I look over at him and raise an eyebrow in question. "You know the one where you are going to try to bed her."

"You don't think I can fuck her tonight?" I ask looking over at him.

"Fuck no man. That bitch has pure virgin written all over her." He starts to laugh and I get an idea.

"A G says I can bed her tonight. That I'll have

her begging me to fuck her for weeks to come." He grins and shakes my hand.

"Deal, motherfucker." We shake on it, I grab my beer that the prospect just delivered, and I make my way towards the girls.

Leaning up against the bar next to her, I give Trixie a smile. "Hey babe, who's your friend?" She gives me a grin in return and introduces me to her shy friend.

"Baby, this is Harlyn. She's a sweet girl who doesn't need your wolf-like stare. You'll scare the poor girl." She raises an eyebrow at me, but I don't let that hinder my curiosity.

"Harlyn." I let her name roll off my tongue as I reach a hand out to her. She gives me a shy smile and places her small hand inside of my larger one. "It's so great to meet you." I kiss her knuckles and I see the blush creep up her cheeks. She dips her head and when she looks back at me, I can see that she's curious about me, too.

"Prez." Trixie warns me, but I don't even care what she says. I have my sights set on Harlyn and there is nothing that will get to me change my mind. "She's the daughter of--" Harlyn smacks her arm and gives her a look before looking back at me. The daughter of who? Now I'm even more intrigued.

Someone calls Trixie, and she reluctantly walks

away from us. Moving closer to Harlyn, I run my hand down her cheek and she moves closer to me. "What is a sweet girl like you doing in a place like this?" I catch a strand of her hair and wrap it around my finger.

"I wanted to live on the edge a little. I've never..." She trails off and then looks away before she looks back at me.

"How old are you sweetheart?" I need to at least make sure she's legal before I fuck her into tomorrow.

"Eighteen." She says too quickly. I look into her eyes and I know she's lying.

"Truth, babe." She looks panicked, but I encourage her to give me the answer.

"Seventeen." She looks down towards the ground and I groan. Of course she has to be a fucking kid still. I don't like corrupting little girls, but damn every ounce of my body is craving her.

"Come with me." I murmur. She looks frightened at first, but I lean in and whisper in her ear. "Don't worry, I won't hurt you." She nods and grabs my outstretched hand. Leading her towards the hallway where the rooms branch out, we walk in silence. When we come to my room, she tenses up next to me. Opening the door, I lead her inside, and lock the door behind us.

She stands in the middle of my room and I want

so bad to strip her down naked and fuck her, but I don't. I stand my ground and just watch the scared little baby bird standing in front of me. "What is a seventeen year old girl doing in my club?" Her cheeks and ears turn red, and she looks sway from me.

"I want to know what it's like." I walk closer to her and I see her shiver in anticipation.

"What what's like?" I reach out to touch her and she leans into my touch.

"Anything, everything." She whispers. Pulling her closer to me, I grip her chin and force her face up. She looks eager, and I want so bad to show her what she wants, but I don't want to corrupt this little girl. I'm six years older than her, but I'm not the nice guy she should lose her virginity to. I'm a mean son of a bitch and I don't give a shit who I hurt.

"As much as I want to corrupt you, I can't. You need a nice man to do that shit. I fuck hard, and rough, that's definitely what a sweet little girl like you needs." She doesn't let me scare her away and I'm intrigued.

"I'm not as innocent as you think." She's getting a little more courageous and I feel my dick twitch with each word she breathes.

"What's the most you've ever done with a man?" I raise an eyebrow at her and she blushes. She doesn't answer my question, so I know that it isn't much. "You ever have a man put his mouth here?" My free hand cups her tit, and she swallows nervously. She shakes her head no and I move my hand to another spot. "What about here?" My hand slides up her skirt and cups her pussy. Her head shakes, and I feel her body tremble.

She's too pure for me to take. I don't have a lot of fuckin' standards, but I don't want to be the one to ruin her. Her body tenses when I run my finger over her panties and her eyes widen. "Have you ever been kissed by a man?" She shakes her head no, so I slam my mouth down on hers in a bruising manner. She whimpers in my mouth and run my tongue over her lips, begging for entrance.

Romeo comes up to me and slaps me on the back. "Well that could have went worse." He has a grin on his face, and I want to beat the fuck out of him.

"Yeah, well you knew Harlyn was here so why'd you let Delilah in? You knew it would cause shit."

"Because I like to watch you sweat." Shaking my head at him, I walk over towards the bar. Mick gets me a beer and places it in front of me. "How you going to get her to stay this time?" he grins, and I just stare at my beer bottle like it's the most interesting thing I've seen lately.

"I'm going to tell her the truth about the shit that went down before." He turns his attention to me and looks around before leaning in.

"You sure? That goes against the fucking club. We don't tell women shit for a reason." He growls.

"She deserves to know why I did what I did. I let her go thinking that she would forgive me, but she didn't, and now with the threat over her head, I ain't letting anything happen to her. The truth just might keep her safe."

"You're a fucking idiot. Nothing is going to change how that girl feels about you. I told you from day one that she wasn't strong enough to be part of this life. She was never fucking right for you, and you just had to prove me wrong." I push off the bar and turn towards my VP.

"Don't fuckin' say another word about her. I don't give a shit if you approve of my ol' lady or not. She's the only one I'll ever have, and she's stronger than every fucking bitch in this place. No one can put up with my shit like she can. She fucking calms me down and without that, who the fuck knows what I would do." He scoffs at that, but he doesn't say anything.

"You're just fucking pussy whipped and you ain't

even getting a piece of her anymore." Before I can stop myself, I take a swing at him and clock him in the jaw. He stumbles into the bar and I lean in to whisper in his ear.

"Don't ever disrespect my ol' lady. I don't give a shit what you say about me, but you say something else about her, and VP or not, I won't think twice about putting a bullet in you." I push off of him and walk towards my room. Looking up, I see Harlyn standing there with wide eyes. I keep walking towards her and I grab her hand, dragging me behind her. We make it into my room and I slam the door shut.

She doesn't say anything for the longest time, and at this point I don't even give a fuck. I'm pissed because my right hand man is questioning my decisions, and I'm even more pissed because I don't know what exactly to do about Harlyn. If she doesn't listen to me, I'll have to fucking lock her ass up in this room like a damn prisoner, and I don't want to. I want her to willingly come to me every God damn night like she used to. I don't want her to spit insults at me every time we are in the same fuckin' room.

"Stav." Her voice is barely above a whisper. I stand rooted to the ground, clenching and unclenching my hands as I try to keep from lashing out at her next.

She moves in closer and she reaches out to put her hand on my cheek. It takes her a second to put her hand on my skin, but when she does, I feel like I can breathe - like maybe the darkness won't take me away this time. My anger has always been a problem for me, and if provoked enough, I fly off the damn handle. It's one of the reasons she left before. Last time it was bad, I killed a man right in front of her. I could hear her screams in my ears, but I couldn't stop what I was doing.

Instead, I dug my knife into that bastard's body and took my time tearing him limb from limb. Not once have I ever regretted killing someone. I'll never regret killing him. I only regret letting her see that side of me. If I would have known that it would be the end of us, I would have had one of my men take her away until it was over.

Chapter Four

"Stavros." Her hand cups my cheek and I close my eyes. "Please look at me." Her voice is soft, and I take a few deep breathes before I open my eyes again. When I don't look at her, she moves to stand in front of me and grabs my cheeks in both of her tiny hands. "Stavros." She says with a little more force.

Blinking, I look down at her and see the concern written all over her face. Wrapping my arms around her small body, I see the fear in her eyes before she quickly masks it again. I don't know why I do it, but I carry her to the bed, and lay us both down.

She doesn't move from her position, and I'm glad. Having her warmth against me makes all the demons fade away. My head is on her chest, and I can't help but run my fingers over the tattoo on the inside of her wrist. It's the tattoo she got when I claimed her as my ol' lady.

Her hands go to the back of my head and she runs her fingers through my hair. "Stavros, you're scaring me." Not moving from my position on her chest, I continue to take deep breaths. Her scent is calming me faster than anything else can. She didn't know the monster I really was when we met, and she's only seen it in very low doses a few times. She hated what I became the last week we were together, and she resented me for being the man she fell in love with.

"I never want to scare you." I finally get the words out. I want her to still be the only one I go to when I need to be calmed down like this.

"What is wrong, Stav?" Her question is so simple, but so difficult.

"Romeo was talking about you. I can deal with him saying shit about me, but when it comes to you…" I trail off. I don't want to freak her out any more than I already am. She deserves the truth, but I don't want her to run because of it - again.

"What did he say?"

"That you weren't strong enough for this life. Pretty much that I'm pussy whipped by you, and you've never been right for me." She doesn't say anything at first, but she does continue to run her fingers through my hair.

"What do you think?"

"I think that you are the strongest woman I know. You've dealt with a lot of my bullshit over the years, and you're the only woman who can calm me." She puts her hand over mine that is still tracing my name on her wrist.

"Yeah I have dealt with your bullshit and that was because I loved you. I would do it all again." She looks down at me, and I can tell she didn't mean to give me that tid bit of information. "I just… I just can't know what you do to those people. What happens when your sins come to haunt us? What happens to me when something happens to you?"

Looking into her eyes, I can see all the doubt and hurt I've given to her. It's my fault that we are where we are, and I want to fuckin' make things right. I don't care what I have to do to prove to her that what we have is the real deal. I was her first everything and she was my first in all the things that mattered. She was the first woman to ever own my heart, warm my bed for more than one night, and to have my brand on her body. No one else will ever fill those roles. Only her. "Harlyn, I never meant for you to see that shit. I should have sent you with one of my men, but I could only think about shoving my knife so deep into his throat that nothing else mattered. He hurt you. He deserved to die."

"You hurt me. Does that mean you deserve the

same thing?" Her statement is like a punch to the gut. I hurt her. I never physically hurt her, but I did do a number on her.

"I will never change the way I am. If a man is going to put his hands on you, I won't hesitate to kill the bastard. That fucker had you tied up to a damn chair and you were bleeding. He almost cut one of your damn arteries. He would have fuckin' killed you if I didn't get there in time. I can't apologize for what I did to him. I would do it again if I had to. I will always protect you." She sucks in a breath at my mention of her being kidnapped. I went fucking postal, and the only way I would be able to sleep at night was by gutting that fucker like a damn pig.

"I did it all for you. I wouldn't have thought twice. Harlyn…" My words begin to fade. I don't even know what to say to her anymore. She thinks I'm a monster and that may be true, but I would do anything to save her.

"I knew you'd find me. You always did. And as much as I hate it, I'm thankful because you saved me. But I still don't want to live in fear. What happens when the next time you have a blackout, you actually hurt me. You scared the shit out of me. I never knew someone could do something as violent as what you did." She blows out a breath and looks down at my hand that's covering my name.

Her lips turn up into a smile and she reaches

down and moves my hand, replacing it with her own finger. She traces the ink and then looks up at me. "Do you remember the day I got this?" Closing my eyes, I listen to her heart beating.

Six months after we met, Harlyn turned eighteen and she had still been coming around the clubhouse to see me the whole damn time. When Romeo looked over at me, he shook his head. I told him that I would have her coming back for more, but the one thing I didn't know was that tonight she was coming back to get what she's tried to get me to do for months.

She had seen me with a club whore a few days after we met. The bitch was taking my cock into her mouth when Harlyn came around the corner. When our eyes met, I could see how angry she was with me. But she didn't have any claim on me and I was still chasing tail just like I would any other day of the week. Just because I had her begging me to take her virginity every day didn't mean shit to me. I couldn't fuck her as long as she was underage.

We both watched her strut in with a dress that was so tight, that it left little to the imagination. Last week in church I had to fucking claim her in order to keep my men from staring at her too long. Every time I turned my back, one of them was going up to her trying to take her to bed. There was no way in fuckin' hell that I would let that happen. I was going to be her first and I didn't care who I had to maim in order to keep her pure.

"Stav." She purrs when she comes up to me. Her hand goes to my bicep and she looks up at me like I hung the moon. I've taken her to bed with me a few times, but all we've done is fool around. I wanted to get her ready to take my dick. She was the tightest little fucking thing I've ever had my fingers in, and I was craving the day that I could finally fuck her.

"Hey baby." I greet her. She leans forward and grabs the back of my neck, and pulls me closer to her.

"Guess what happens at midnight." She had a wide smile and I took the bait. Wrapping my arm around her waist, I pull her body into mine and ask her what. "I turn eighteen." I groan at her words. It's something I've been fucking waiting for what seems like forever. I finally get to feel her sweet little cunt squeezing my dick.

"Is that what this getup is for?" I ask eyeing her dress.

"No, this is for you." She beams at me. She has come a long damn way from the scared little girl I met a few months ago. Openly flirting with me, wasn't something that I pictured her doing, but my god she's a fuckin' natural at it.

Picking her up bridal style, I tell Romeo that I'm heading in for the night and I carry her to my room. She giggles and places kisses along my neck that cause my dick to grow in my jeans. Fuck, her mouth feels even better than before.

When I drop her on my bed, I can see the lust in her eyes. Every damn thing about her is fuckin' perfect and I'm one lucky son of a bitch to have found her. Yeah I've fucked things up between us a time or two, but she still came back. I never lied to her about what I would be doing when she wasn't here. My dick was my property and there wasn't anyone that could change that - or so I thought.

Before I could even get on the bed with her, she surprises me with a question. "Why don't you have an ol' lady?" Sitting on the edge of the bed, I look over at her and try to figure out where this shit is coming from.

"Because I like to fuck who I want, when I want." Moving so I can crawl over to her on the bed, I see a little flash of hurt fill her expression before it disappears just as quickly as it appeared.

"So after you fuck me, that's it?" I've already told her that I didn't do the clingy bitches who wanted something from me. I liked being alone because that meant that no one else had to deal with the monster that I had inside of me. Sometimes, there was nothing I could do to stop the beast from coming out. Something in my head just changed and I didn't even know who I was. I didn't want to subject someone else to that.

"I didn't say that. You are different than every other bitch I've even messed around with. I like being with you." I place a kiss on her lips and she wraps her arms around me.

"Fuck me." She whispers against my lips. Dropping my head, I close my eyes and when I open them again, she's looking up at me. She has that look of lust on her face. Looking at the clock on the wall, I see that there are only a few more hours until midnight. What's a few hours going to hurt. She came here knowing what she was doing.

"Let's make a deal." I nip at her neck, and hold her hands above her head.

"What are you proposing?" The slight hint of interest at my words is written all over her face, and I have a feeling that she will do anything I ask her to.

"You put my name on your body and I'll fuck you before midnight." She looks at me for a second before she says anything.

"Doesn't that..." She trails off and her brows pull together in question. I know what it means, and I have a feeling she does, too. When I take her, I know that there is no fuckin' way that I'll let another man have her.

I will kill anyone who even tries to take what's mine.

"Yes or no, babe. It's not a hard decision. You want me to fuck you tonight, then you put my name on you. You'll be mine and only mine." Harlyn's eyes roam down my body and I know she's trying to picture me naked again. She's seen my body before, and she knows how big my dick is. I don't know why she's wasting time.

"Yes." Her answer is quiet, but she looks determined.

"Once I have you baby, I won't give you up." Her eyes meet mine and she doesn't look nervous anymore.

"I like the sound of that." Leaning down, I press my lips to hers. She spreads her legs as much as she can and I move both of her wrists into one of my hands above her head. I use my other hand to slide her dress up so I can fit in between her thighs. She wraps her long legs around me, and her heels dig into my ass.

Pulling away from her, breathless, I grab her hand and pull her off the bed with me. We have a pit stop before I deflower my little virgin.

"It definitely wasn't romantic like you deserved."
I state, still rubbing her wrist. "I did it because I wanted
every fucker who tried to put his hands on you to know
who you belonged to."

"You are just a modern version caveman, Stav.
You gave me a choice that day and I made the
decision. I wanted you. Hell, I wanted every part of you
that you were willing to give me. I knew you had your
issues, but you never once took advantage of me. You
treated me like I was the most important thing in your
life." She leans forwards and her lips brush over my
forehead.

"That's because you are." Instead of trying to
think of the best way to put this, I just tell her. "You are
the only one who can bring me down to my knees. You
hold this power over me and the whole time you've
been gone, I could only think about you, and what you
were doing, and who you were with. I had to fuckin'
stop myself more times than I could count from going to
you and bringing your ass back here." She presses her
forehead against mine and closes her eyes.

"I never slept with them." My head snaps up to

hers and I see the truth in her eyes.

"Then…" I don't know what to even say. My man that was following her said that she was taking men home with her, and going to their places.

"I know you had someone follow me. It's probably why you let me stay away for so long." She pauses and reaches down to grab my hand. When she continues, I'm speechless. "I made it look like I was sleeping with other people so that your man would tell you. I wanted you to hurt as bad as I did."

Chapter Five

Hearing the truth fall from her lips is almost as painful as it is exultant. My anger takes a hold of me instead of focusing on the happiness I should be feeling that I'm the only one who's ever been inside of her. Pulling my head away from her, I grip her throat. It isn't enough to hurt her, and it sure as hell isn't doing anything to tame the beast that's rising in me. Her hands get out of my grip and they go to my forearm.

"Stav." She's the only one I let call me that. She's the only one that I've given my heart to, and she intentionally tried to fuck with my head. My fingers start to squeeze her neck, but she never shows me fear. "Stavros. Please look at me." I close my eyes because I can't look at her. If I do, I won't be able to stay mad at her. Her voice softens and I want to kiss her. "I can't breathe." She mumbles.

Releasing her, I get off of her and the bed, making my way into the bathroom. Looking in the mirror at myself, I don't see that man she fell in love with. She's right; she deserves a fuckin' better life than the one I can give her. Slamming my hand into the mirror, I welcome the pain as pieces of glass slice through my skin. The pieces fall into the sink and the ground, but I don't even give a fuck. Warm red blood starts to drip down my hand and into the sink basin.

"Stav." She gasps. She comes over to me and when her body brushes mine, I get a glimpse of our past. The sweet touches, the sultry glances, the nights that we spent wrapped up in each other.

She grabs a towel and holds it to my hand to clean up some of the blood from my skin. I watch her dark hair fall into her face as she gently starts to pull the towel away. I feel a pinch when she moves her hands away from mine, and I see a shard of glass still sticking in my skin. When she goes to pull the glass out, I grit my teeth. She looks up at me as she pulls it out, and I can see that her seeing me like this is hurting her. Every fuckin' thing I do anymore hurts her. Maybe she's right. Maybe letting her go is probably the only thing that is going to save her.

"Do you have anything to clean this out with?" I pull my hand away from her and she frowns. She grabs my hand and pulls it back to her. "Don't start being a dick. I see you even when you're trying to push me away. If I don't clean this out it's going to get infected.

Who the fuck knows when you last cleaned this mirror." She stares at me with the sassy look I love, and I give in to her.

"Check under the sink." I rasp out. Watching her bend down to look under the seat, my head swims with ideas of what I want to do to her again. Images of her spread out for me on our bed, the way she held me as I fucked her on my bike, and when I installed the sex swing in our bedroom, and fucked her long and hard.

As she stands back up, I see the tattoo peek out from under her shirt; it says my club name, Draconic Crimson. She got it a few months before she left. She wanted me to know that no matter what happened between us, she would always be on my side. What a crock of shit that turned out to be.

When the shit hits my hand, I grunt out in displeasure. "Next time you do that, you better suck my dick to keep my mind off the damn burning in my hand." I grumble. She looks up at me and shakes her head.

"I swear, you still haven't changed a bit. I probably would've bit your dick just to piss you off." Grabbing a strand of her hair, I wrap it around my finger and give it a tug. Her eyes meet mine and she gives me a challenging look.

"You can act like you don't want my dick babe, but I know that it's the only thing you've been thinking about since I fucked you on my desk." She snorts and pours more shit on my hand causing me to pull away from her.

"Don't assume shit. I may want your dick, but that's all I want from you." She pulls my hand back to her and starts to wrap it in a bandage. When she's done, she slaps her hand down on it, and I grab the back of her neck before she can even flinch.

Pulling her body flush against mine, I feel the way her body melts into me. I still make her feel things about me. "I'm going to let you make up your own mind. I'm going to give you the facts, and then you can decide what to do with it. Just know that if someone else puts their hands on you, I'll kill them."

Harlyn bites her lip and then nods her head. "The Fighting Rebels will do everything in their power to get you. They want to get back at me because I let one of my men still their prez's ol' lady right from under his nose. He had been beating the fuck out of her, and when my man found her, he protected her. They fuckin' ended up falling in love. I don't give a fuck what they do, but I do protect my own, and once he claimed her, she became my responsibility. Now Flint wants you. An eye for an eye type of fucking shit. He knows you're my fucking weakness. You're my only weakness."

Her eyes widen, but she doesn't say anything to me yet. "He told me that when he found you, he would make sure that he didn't take it easy on you. I saw what his ol' lady looked like when she was brought here, and trust me, it isn't something that many women can live through. To be honest, I'm surprised she didn't die from a few of her injuries." Pulling away from her body, I make my way out of the bathroom, and take a seat on the bed. She doesn't move from the doorway of the bathroom, but her eyes are focused on me.

"How does he even know about me? I thought you said that it was never going to leave the club?" she looks angry and it turns me on.

"Baby, we went out in public and practically fucked everywhere. I didn't leak any important information for a reason. I needed you safe unless…" Harlyn crosses the room, and takes a seat on the bed next to me.

"Unless what?" she places her hand on mine and intertwines our fingers together.

"They are trying to get me to take him out. A lot of people know how fucking ruthless I am when someone tries to hurt someone I care about. They are probably baiting me to kill him for even thinking of touching you." Getting up, I make my way towards the door without looking back at her.

Before I can make it out the door, she grabs the back of my shirt and doesn't release me. Turning to face her, I can see something new in her eyes. Something I haven't seen in over a year. Love. "What are you going to do? You're not going after him are you?" Her voice cracks and that's the only way I know that it's affecting her. I don't know why she cares if I go after him if she doesn't even want to be with me. The faster I get this done, the faster she'll get what she wants – her freedom.

"I'll do whatever it takes to make sure you're protected. I know you don't want this life, and as much as I want to lock you up in here, I won't do that. I promised you happiness, and if I don't give it to you anymore, then I'll give you your freedom instead." Tears start to fill her eyes, but I can't take it anymore. Opening the door, I make my way out before I give her one last look. She's biting her lip again, and I want to go to her, but I don't. Instead, I shut the door and make my way towards the bar where my men are all gathered.

When I walk over to them, I see the look on Romeo's face. He's pissed at me, but we've been friends for years. He's knows what to not say to me, and I'm sure he knew it was coming before I even hit him.

"Church." I growl. All the men turn towards me and they don't say a word. They just make their way towards the doors and walk inside. Romeo is still leaning against the bar and I just know he wants to say something.

"I get it Stavros, but you need to get your fucking head on straight. That girl makes you fucking crazy, and I won't watch you destroy yourself over her. She either wants in this life again, or she wants out. She needs to decide once and for all. This shit won't fly again." He straightens and then walks towards church.

Looking towards the hall, I see Harlyn peeking around the corner. Motioning for her to come to me, I wait. When she gets close enough, I wrap an arm around her waist. "He doesn't like me." I shake my head no and then I see Romeo standing at the door watching us. Her eyes follow mine to him and she frowns. "I don't want to make things harder for you. I will stay out of your way until you deal with whatever it is that you need to."

Her face tells me that she wants to say more, but she holds her tongue. "Go back to the room. I'll come for you when I'm done." She nods her head and stands on her tip toes that make her almost reach my lips. Her mouth presses against mine, and she slips her tongue into my mouth. Wrapping my hand around the back of her head, I pull her into me.

As I pull away from her, I look down in her eyes. "I'll see you in a little while."

Making my way towards church, I see the look in Romeo's eyes. "Does that mean she's staying?" I shrug my shoulder and walk past him. Taking my seat at the head of the table, I wait for Romeo to close the door and take his seat next to me. Slamming the gavel on the table, I wait a second before I speak.

"I'm sure everyone already knows that Harlyn is back. I pulled her back into our protection because of the threat that Flint and the Fighting Rebels are out to make her pay for the sins of our brother." The whole table looks over at Slink. He looks down and shakes his head.

"Prez, I never meant –" I hold my hand up, cutting him off.

"Don't worry about it brother. I promised you protection and I won't go back on my word." He doesn't say anything in response to my words, but he does nod his head at me. "I know a few of you are pissed off that she's here, but I will be making sure that she's protected. I've been waiting for her to come back since the day she left, and I won't take any of your guy's shit."

I look over at Romeo and he has a dirty look on his face. "What are we doing to keep them at bay?" One of the new guys asks.

"We go on lock down. You have twenty-four hours to bring everyone in. I won't stand for anyone running their mouth and causing shit. If your ol' ladies don't like the whores, they need to keep their mouths shut." I watch the guys around the table nod their heads and I slam the gavel on the table again, dismissing them.

The room clears and the only ones left are me, Romeo, and Dex. "Prez, the word on the street is they know she's here. Should we be gearing up for a war?"

Romeo looks over at me and we don't even have to say anything to get on the same page. "Gear up. We need the gun storage packed to the brink, and up the security. Oh, and get a few of the guys to load up on some food. Not sure how long we are going to be keeping everyone here, but we need to be prepared."

Romeo nods his head before adding something else. "No one is allowed to leave the clubhouse alone. I know the men are going to bitch, but I don't want to take any chances. The Fighting Rebels don't give a fuck who they hurt in the process of this war. Families aren't to leave, period." Dex nods his head, and goes to stand up.

When he walks through the door, I turn to my VP and grip the edge of the table. "You think they are stupid enough to try and storm the place?" He sounds on edge, but you wouldn't be able to tell by his demeanor.

"Depends on how bad he wants her." I look towards the door even though I know that none of the guys are going to come through it.

"Every member of our club is on the line right now, plus all of their families, all over one girl." He narrows his eyes and I clench and unclench my hand.

"No, there are two women that fucker wants, and I'll be damned if I let him get close to either one. I will not let anyone try to intimidate us." He nods his head and leans back in his chair.

"You still love her."

"Never stopped. She could have tried to fucking kill me in my sleep and I'd still crave her. She is the only fucking thing that makes me calm. You've seen how fucking antsy I've been since she's been gone." He nods, looking down at his hands.

"I watched you kill the bastard she was sleeping with after she left. You know when she finds out, she's going to be fucking pissed. That shit isn't fucking normal. You two are like fuckin' oil and water."

"She won't find out." I grit out. There are a lot of things that I regret, and that was one of them. I couldn't squash the fucking pain in my chest until it was too late. The monster in me took over, and I couldn't stop myself.

Chapter Six

Making my way into my room, I see Harlyn under my covers with her eyes closed. It's a little after midnight, and instead of waking her up, I just strip down and slide in behind her. I'm sure she will give me nothing but shit when she wakes up, but I can't bring myself to give a fuck. It's not like I'll be sleeping anywhere else.

Wrapping my arm around her waist, I pull her smaller body into mine, and I can feel her bare legs against me. She moves around a couple times before she settles in and relaxes.

I don't fall asleep right away because I like being able to hold her. Thinking back to the last time she was in my arms, I can't help but smile.

One Year, Six Months, Six Hours Ago

"Stav! Stop tickling me!" She gasps. I roll us over and she straddles my waist. Her cheeks are flush and she looks like a hot mess. Tonight's my birthday, and she surprised me at the clubhouse with a tiny little outfit covered in my leather jacket. She strutted into the clubhouse with no shame. Every one of my men had their eyes on her, but she only had eyes for me.

"How about you get to work on giving me my birthday present, babe." I smirk at her and she grins. She slowly slides down my body until her face is hovering over my dick. I watch as her pink tongue slips out of her mouth and slowly licks the tip. Her mouth slides over my tip, and slowly sinks down. She takes me to the back of her throat, and I can feel her tongue as she continues to massage the underside of my dick.

Every bob of her head brings me closer to the edge. My hands roam her body before they tangle in her hair. My dick hardens further, so I start to move her head to a speed I want. Thrusting my hips up, I shove my dick so far down her throat that she starts to gag. Every noise she makes brings me to the edge until I shoot my cum in her mouth. I slow my hips as I ride out my orgasm, and my fingers tighten in her hair.

When I pull her off my dick, I see the lust in her eyes. I pull her naked body up mine, and she straddles me again. Before I can even get her ready to take me in her sweet cunt, she's already gliding down my shaft. Every time she slides up and down me is like pure fuckin' magic.

Her hands roam down her own body and I love that she gets more adventurous every time we have sex. I watch as her fingers rub her clit in small, little circles. Her mouth forms and O and she drops her head back. "Stav. Oh God." My fingers run up her body and I pinch one of her nipples. She looks down at me and her eyes are blazing with a heat that no one can question.

"I love you." I grunt out. I thrust in and out of her at a quick pace. Her sweet cunt just about squeezes the shit out of me.

She leans forward and claims my mouth. "I love you too Stav." Just hearing her words brings me over the edge. Grabbing her neck, I give it a light squeeze and she digs her fingernails into my chest. We come together, and she falls down on my chest, huffing out for a breath.

She slowly slides up and off of my dick, and falls onto the bed next to me. Turning her head towards me, she gives me a small grin. "Happy birthday, baby." She turns away from me and I cuddle up behind her, pulling her ass into my dick.

On nights where she's feeling extra frisky, after a little alcohol, she lets me fuck her ass. Now that would have been a fuckin' great way to bring in the start of twenty-seven.

Falling asleep with her just like this is the only way that I am able to keep the demons at bay. Just her innocence keeps me sane. Without her by my side, I don't know what I would do, or who I would become.

Waking up the next morning, I feel her grinding back into me. Her hand is absently running up and down my thigh. My dick is pressed firmly between the perfect globes of her ass as she slides it up and down my length. My hand is itching to wrap around her neck as I sink into her from behind. Her moan fills the room and her fingers dig into my leg where they were just at.

Unable to control myself, I wrap my fingers around her neck, and pull her upper body towards my chest. Her head rests against my chest and when I look down at her, she has her eyes closed and her mouth open.

Harlyn has always been a kinky bitch and I never think twice when I give it to her. She takes what I dish out with no complaints, unless she's telling me to fuck her harder. Thrusting my hips into her, I put a little pressure on her throat and I feel her tighten around me. "Stav, please fuck me harder." Her whimpers and moans make me harder.

Flipping her over onto her stomach, I pull her ass in the air and line myself up before slamming into her. Each thrust is hard, and rough. Her hands are tangled in the blankets and she can't move. Pushing her lower back down, I get her arched in the perfect position. My balls slap against her, and with each thrust she's moaning louder. Grabbing the back of her hair, I pull her head towards me and I kiss along her neck.

Sinking my teeth into the skin of her neck, she whimpers. Our skin is covered in a thin layer of sweat, and I'm thrusting into her like the fucking world is ending and I want to come before it does. Our breathing is hard, and I release her to grab onto her hips. Slamming her body back onto mine works me up faster than ever before, and I can't stop the orgasm that hits. Filling her with my cum makes the jealous asshole that I am, beat on his chest. I want everyone to know that I'm the only one who's ever came inside of her sweet little cunt.

She will never know what another man feels like.

And if she does, I won't let him see the next day. Call me crazy, but I don't fucking care. She's mine, and if I can't have her, no one will.

I pull out of her slowly and she collapses on the bed in front of me. Looking down at her beautiful body, I can't help but grin when I see what she's got on. She has a "Property of Draconic Crimson" shirt. Her sexy ass is barely peeking out from under it, and if she's willing to wear a property shirt, then she'll be willing to be back under me, and on the back of my bike.

My eyes scan the length of her body and when she looks up at me, I can see a grin on her lips. "Like what you see?" She has a hint of sarcasm in her voice, but I don't let that distract me. The only thing I can think about is my property tattoo on her body, and my name on her wrist.

"You know I like what I see. I wouldn't have made you my ol' lady if I didn't." She gives me a dirty look over her shoulder, and wiggles her ass in the air.

"You only made me your ol' lady so that none of your men would try and fuck me first." She lays flat on the bed and I lean over her. My dick slides along her body as I come to hover over her.

"I made you my ol' lady because I'm a selfish bastard, and I am not sharing you with anyone. You're mine, and no one will ever touch what's mine." She huffs out a breath, but doesn't turn around. Her words are almost too low for me to hear.

"Yeah, apparently. That's probably why no man would even try to get too close. And the ones who did weren't you. The minute they put their hands on me, I couldn't help but compare them to you. You're such a bastard. You should have sent me away when I was seventeen. But no, you wanted to keep me for yourself. All but drag me through the hell you were going through."

Flipping her over, I lean down and get in her face. "You're the only reason I was able to fucking survive that hell I went through. Without you, I would have given up years ago. You fucking saved me." My eyes go to the scar on her neck, and I think back to when I found her in that fuckin' warehouse with that son of a bitch who left a scar on her perfect skin.

My men have been searching for hours. I knew I shouldn't have let her go out with the girls tonight. I had a sick feeling in my gut that something was going to happen, but I didn't listen to it. She gave me her pouty fuckin' lips, and sucked my dick. I gave in.

Grabbing my phone for the hundredth fucking time, I call Dex and ask him for a status report. They have to have heard something by now. We don't fucking pay shit loads of money to these cops and their associates to not a have a damn thing on them.

"They haven't heard shit. I'm trying to get a lock on her phone GPS, but haven't had luck. Who would have taken her? Who did we piss off this time?" Instead of even answering him, I end the call and grit my teeth. We are straight with everyone right now. There isn't any reason for anyone to even think about coming after her.

My phone starts to ring, and when I put it to my ear, I hear her whimpers. "Stavros Levin." My blood runs cold and I motion for Romeo to come over. He stops what he's doing, and I pull the phone away from my ear and put it on speaker.

"Who the fuck is this?" I growl. The sound of something hitting flesh breaks through the phone and I hear her cry out in pain.

"Now, now. I don't want you to say the wrong thing and cause this pretty little girl anymore pain than I already have planned for her. I knew you were a tough son of a bitch to track down and get close to, but I finally found the perfect way to get even with you." Clenching my fists, I try to keep the beast from taking over and tearing this whole damn town apart looking for her. I will kill anyone who gets in my fuckin' way. Consequences be damned. Teddy. We've had our beefs before, but this goes even deeper than that. A year ago, I stole half a mil in guns from him and he's been looking for me ever since.

"You fuckin' hurt her and I'll hunt you down like the fuckin' dog you are. I don't give a fuck what I have to do. You are fuckin' dead." He hangs up before I can say anything else, but it doesn't matter. I know where I'm heading, and he better hope like fuckin' hell that he isn't still there when I show up. Having his blood on my hands is the only way that I'll be able to calm the beast. He threatened my ol' lady, and he has her. I heard her cry out in pain. I'm the only one who gets to put my hands on her.

Making it to the warehouse faster than I've ever thought possible, I dismount my bike, and grab my knife out of the holder at my side. The guys follow my lead, but I'm not thinking straight. As soon as I get sight of that bastard, I'm going for the fuckin' jugular.

My men open the doors and we all file inside, spreading out to take all sides of the building. They already know I'm out for blood, and they won't stop me until I get what I came for. Getting through the second door, I see her tied to a damn chair. She has blood on her face and her eye is swollen. There is a cut running down her cheek, but it doesn't look all that deep. Her clothes are torn, and she looks nothing like she did when I dropped her off at the club with the girls.

I notice movement out of the corner of my eye

and I take my eyes off of her for a minute. "Stav." My name falls from her lips on a broken whisper. Making my way towards her, I don't give a fuck what happens to me as long I get her to safety. I won't go down without a fight. I barely get her untied before I hear Romeo yell out my name. When I turn, I get a knife to the shoulder. Harlyn yelps, and I launch myself at him.

Red is all I see when I straddle this fucker. I deliver blow after blow to him. Romeo pulls me off of him, and sends me back, but I can't stay away. Before I turn around, I hear her whimper again. When I look behind me, that fucker's moved, and he has her in his grip with a knife at her throat. I don't even think twice, I run at them both, and he pushes her away. Taking him down, I fight with him over the knife and I end up pushing it through his chest. But I don't stop there. I pull it out and gut the mother fucker like a fish.

Blood curling screams fill the warehouse. I don't even notice the blood that is now covering almost every inch of my body. Her screams sound like they're far away and when I turn around, I see a look on her face that I'll never forget.

Disgust. Hatred. Fear. Love. Hurt.

Her good eye scans the scene in front of her, but she doesn't move. Instead Romeo grabs her, and pulls her towards the door. I'm not done with this fucker and I know if she sees any more, she'll hate me even more than she thinks she does right now.

I take my time with him. Now that I don't have an audience, I don't care how fuckin' loud he screams as I dig his own knife into his skin.

chapter Seven

Reaching forward, I run my finger over one of the scars that she was left with after that night. At first she flinches, but then she sinks back into the mattress. "How long do I have to stay here?" The question is nothing more than a question, but it feels like a knife is being shoved into my chest. Laying on the bed next to her, I look up at the ceiling.

"Once we deal with the Fighting Rebels, you can go." The words come out harsher than I intended, but I can't bring myself to really give a fuck. Instead of sitting in the silence with her, I get out of bed, and make my way to my dresser. Pulling out a pair of jeans, I pull them on and grab my boots. When I look over my shoulder, I see her watching me intently. When her eyes meet my tattoo, I see them widen.

Not long after she left, I got a tattoo that reminded me of her. This way, no matter how far apart we were, she would always be with me. Grabbing a tee shirt, I pull it over my head and pull on my cut. Before I make it out the door, she stops me.

"Stavros." Her voice glues me to the spot I'm standing. Looking over my shoulder at her, I see the questioning look.

"It only means as much as the person it was designed after." I don't say anything else; I just walk out of the room, and let her think about it.

I had this designed for her, and only her. It's one of the only tattoos on my body that has a true meaning. It holds a promise and curse all at the same time. I'm bound to her in ink, just like she's bound to me.

Walking into the bar area, I see a bunch of people gathering around. Families are starting to arrive, and the prospects are starting to unload boxes of shit that they got at the store. Hopefully it's enough to hold everyone over for a few days at least. I know I'm going to be sending these fuckers out a dozen or so more times before we even get anything accomplished with the threats that are looming over our heads..

I see Trixie come strutting in with a little dark haired boy on her hip, and I know shit's going to get fuckin' shitty in here. Trixie has been a club whore for a little over six years, and she's slept with every one of the men here. That little boy belongs to one of my men, and when his ol' lady gets here, she's going to know that he's been stepping out on her.

Shit, a bunch of my men have ol' ladies at home, and a whore they fuck here on a daily basis. It isn't my problem, so I don't even bother with the drama. I was never the cheating type. As long as Harlyn was my ol' lady, I never once stepped out on her. She was the only thing I needed, and the only thing that ever got near my dick. Sure the bitches tried on a daily basis, but I had all I needed wrapped in a tight little package that was feisty, kinky, and sexy as fuck.

When she left, sure I started to dip my dick inside the other bitches around here again, but I never made another promise of ol' lady status. Never again will I go down that fucking road unless she steps back up to the plate and reclaims her throne.

"Prez." Red says as he walks over to me.

"Yeah, brother?" I look over his shoulder and see Romeo watching us. He doesn't make a move towards us, but I know that he always sees everything. He's the watcher of the group. That's why I have him as my right hand man. He sees things that others miss.

"I have a feeling my ol' lady is going to cause a fucking scene." I look back at him and his eyes roam until they lock on Chrissy. She's one of the newer whores that started to hang around here.

"She knows?" I ask. I've known about him stepping out on his ol' lady before, but the look on his face says it's something more than just the cheating.

"She found the text messages on my phone one night and I told her to keep her mouth shut here, but you know how bitches are." I nod my head. I already had to deal with Delilah yesterday.

"Keep them away from each other. I don't want more shit going on in here than we can handle." He nods, and I motion for Romeo to come over to us. Red is a good fuckin' kid, but he got married way too fuckin' young. I don't know why he doesn't just cut ties with the bitch, but then again, that isn't my problem. Hell he isn't the only one in that fucking mess. E is in the same damn boat.

Slink walks in the room next with his arm around his ol' ladies neck. She looks ten times better than she did when he brought her here the first time. They make their way towards a few of the other guys, and I turn my attention back to my VP.

"We might have a few angry ol' ladies today." He nods his head and looks around at the men and their families that are already gathered.

"Is there someone else besides Trixie and her boy?"

"Yeah. Red has been stepping out with Chrissy. Plus, we probably haven't heard the last of Delilah." He grins at that. Sometimes I swear he likes to piss me the fuck off.

"What? You're the stupid fucker who stuck your

dick in that pussy, not me." I shake my head and watch a few more people show up. Scanning the room, I see Delilah strut in wearing a skirt so short that her twat is hanging out, and so is her damn ass. Her shirt is tighter than normal, and I can bet that it's because she's trying to get a rise out of me. She almost trips on her fucking shoes and I can't help but laugh.

"That bitch is a walking train wreck." Romeo muses from beside me.

"You have no fucking clue. I can't wait until we are able to get everyone out of this place." A few of the guys come walking up to us, and before I can even say anything, Delilah comes right at me. She jumps into my arms and I hold my hands in the air. Her mouth attacks my face, and when I look at my men, they all have grins on their faces. Pushing her off of me, I watch her ass hit the hardwood floor as she cries out in pain.

"Stay the fuck off me." I growl. She looks up at me and I can see the tears already forming in her eyes. I don't give a fuck. Bitches and tears don't do shit to me. She knows better than to throw her skanky ass on me.

"Stavros." She whines. She stumbles a few times trying to right herself, but only looks more like a fool. "You said that we are together. You said that you'd make me your ol' lady."

My men snicker beside me, and I can't help but

shake my head at her. Leaning towards her, I grab her arm and whisper in her ear. "Stay the fuck away from me, and Harlyn. You so much as come near me or her again and I won't hesitate to put a bullet in you. We clear?"

She jerks out of my grip, and all but runs across the room towards the bar. "That looks like it went well." We all turn towards Harlyn's voice and I can see the satisfaction written all over her face.

"I already told her. Just thought I should reiterate my point." Turning away from her, I focus on my men. "What can I do for you boys?"

Clap and Mirror both look at Harlyn, and then back at me before stating whatever it is they wanted. "Just wanted to let you know that the game room is set up for the kids, and the whores are set to stay in the last room down the hall." I nod my head and they leave.

"So you're just going to ignore me now?" She has no fucking clue what I'd rather do to her right now, but I have a club to run, and we are getting ready for a lock down. Things are more important than what she wants.

"No, I'm busy." I grunt out. I can feel Romeo staring at me, but I don't care. She isn't staying here longer than the lock down so why should I give her the time of day.

"Whatever." She mutters. I feel her walk by me

and I watch her ass shake as she makes her way towards Trixie and her son. As soon as Trixie sees her, she screams out her name and rushes over to her.

"Oh my god! You look so freaking good!" They fall into a fit of hugs and giggles. I watch her eyes light up when she takes a look at the little boy, and my chest constricts. She deserves that and so much more, but I already know that I'm not fit to be a father. Hell, I'm not even fit to be her ol' man.

"Watching you two is like a fucking train wreck. Its fucking gruesome, but you can't look away." Instead of replying to his stupid comment, I make my way towards my office and shut the door. I don't want to deal with this shit. All I want to do right now is drown in a bottle of Johnny.

I end up spending most of the day in my office looking over invoices and shit. By the time dinner rolls around, Trixie comes to the door and asks if I want anything. "No baby, I'm good. Thanks for the offer." I hold the bottle up for her to see, and she shakes her head. She walks in the door and shuts it behind her.

When I look up at her, I can tell she wants to say something, but isn't sure how I'll react. "Just say it, Trix." I sigh, sitting my pen and bottle down on the desk next to me.

"She still loves you." Running my hand down the front of my face, I sit back in my chair and stare at her for a second.

"How would you know?" I know it's a stupid question, but I couldn't help but ask it.

"Because all she can do is talk about you. The whole time you've been in here, she's been scanning the room, just waiting for you to come out. She acts like she hates you for what you did, but she doesn't. She knows that you had to do it in order to protect her. She doesn't get how damn lucky she is. You would give your life up for her, and look at me," she motions to herself. "I've got a kid by a man who will never leave his ol' lady. My son will never know who his father really is because he's a chicken shit bastard. At least Harlyn won't have to worry about whether or not you're going to be that child's father."

Getting up from my spot, I close the distance between us and wrap my arms around her. "I'm sorry he's a fuckin' moron. You deserve better, baby." The door to my office opens and I hear a gasp and then it slams shut again. Closing my eyes, I can feel my anger come back.

When Trix pulls away, she looks like she's sorry. She isn't the one who's taking this out of context, Harlyn is. "I'm sorry if I just made things worse for you."

"Don't worry about it. Just worry about your son. Are you getting money from E?" She shakes her head no and I walk over to my desk and grab an envelope. "I know that this isn't the same as him taking care of his son, but let me help you. I love you like a bratty little sister, and I don't want you or Blade to want for anything."

She shakily takes the envelope from me, and kisses me on the cheek. "I'll pay you back Stavros. I promise." I shake my head, but she grabs my hand and tells me again that she will.

"Okay. Fine." What she doesn't know is that I'll just take the money she gives me and put it in a fund for Blade.

I watch her walk out the door, and she gives me one last sad smile before she goes. Grabbing the bottle of Johnny Blue, I make my way to my room to finish the bottle.

Opening the door, I look in and see that she isn't here yet. I make my way inside, and strip down. As much as I don't want to, my mind starts to replay another happy fucking memory with Harlyn. Sometimes I just wish the damn thing would shut off so I could have some peace.

"I love you." The words that were so meaningless before, now stop my heart. This perfect fuckin' angel in my arms shouldn't love me. She shouldn't even want to be with me, but for some reason she is. She makes my darkest days brighter, and for once, I can actually see myself settling down and having kids with her one day.

"I don't know why you'd love a man like me." I whisper against her lips. They turn up into a smile, and she pushes back from me so she can look into my eyes.

"You're the only person who hasn't treated me differently because they think I'm still just a kid." Her lips are looking pouty and full. I can see the whisker burn on them, and on her neck. My hands run down her back and grip her ass, pressing her body to mine.

"That's because they don't get to experience this sexy body of yours. Yeah baby girl you're young, but, fuck, you take my dick like you've been doing it for years." She pushes at my chest and I can't help but smirk at her.

"That doesn't make me feel better." She pulls away from me and I stop her.

"Baby you are so much more than just a piece of ass for me. You're my whole damn world. I fuckin' love you more than the air I breathe. Without you, I'd suffocate." I watch her expression change from sadness, to happiness, and then to love, in the matter of seconds. She leans down and presses her mouth to mine.

"You make me the happiest I've ever been. If I hadn't met you that night, who knows where I would be right now. You've taken a shy girl and made her feel confident and sexy."

Chapter Eight

Waking up a few hours later, I feel a body slide over mine. I'm so drunk that I can't even see straight, let alone figure out what the fuck is happening. Lips run down my neck, and a hand cups my dick. Closing my eyes, I just let her do what she wants. I don't even fucking care right now. She can use me anyway she wants. I sleep buck naked, so it's not like she needs my help getting me undressed.

When I open my eyes again, I see what I think is blonde hair. I try to blink away the haziness, but it's no fucking use. I hear the door slam against the wall, and screaming fills my room. It sounds like Harlyn is yelling at someone. Before I can even get my head up to look at the doorway, I see a blur of people. It sounds like someone beating the fuck out of someone, but I can't make sense of anything.

The last thing I remember was thinking about the first time Harlyn told me she loved me, and drinking a few big swigs from the bottle of Johnny. The noises quiet down, and I feel her skin press against mine. She cups my face and I groan at the feeling.

"Stav? Can you hear me?" I nod my head, and she runs her thumb over my lips. "That stupid bitch is lucky Romeo pulled me off of her."

"Who?" I rasp out.

"Delilah. I hate that stupid bitch. I hope she gets herpes and dies." Harlyn helps me sit up, and I sway. "How much did you have to drink?" She puts her hand on my forehead and I have a hard time adjusting my eyes to see her.

"Stav you're scaring me. Are you okay?" I shake my head no and it was a fuckin' mistake. My head swims and I fall into her lap.

"Babe." I whisper hoarsely. "I don't feel well."

She gets off the bed and walks out of the room without another word. I can barely hold my head up now and my eyes are getting heavy. What the fuck did that bitch Delilah put in my bottle of Johnny?

The next time I come to, I see a worried frown on Harlyn's face. She's sitting with her back against the wall. Her feet are lying across my body, and she's watching me intently.

"Har." My voice breaks, and she scrambles to sit on her knees next to me.

Her hand runs across my face and I lean into her touch. "What happened?" I ask. Looking around the room, everything looks the same. She grips my hand in hers, and gives it a light squeeze.

"That stupid bitch drugged you. She tried to get you so fucked up that you didn't know who you were fucking last night. Romeo pulled me off of her when they found us in the hall fighting." Looking more closely at her face, I see a scratch and a small bruise that's forming on her jaw. Reaching my arm up, I run my fingertips over her soft skin.

"Thank you." She gives me a sad smile and I pull her down to lay with me. My whole body is weak and I just want to sleep for another twelve hours, or more.

"Last night scared the shit out of me. I had no

idea what was wrong, and when I brought Romeo in here, he called the doc. At some point you stopped breathing." Her voice isn't as strong as it typically is, and she looks worried still. Running my thumb over her knuckles, I feel the scabs that are starting to form on them.

Pulling her hands to my face, I check out the damage. "You do all this to her?" She nods and puts her head on my chest. She doesn't say anything or make any noise, but I can feel her body wrack with silent sobs. Wrapping my arms around her, I hold her until I can't keep my eyes open any longer.

A few hours later, I feel her hands dancing along my bare stomach. Her fingers trail from my chest down to the hair that leads down my pants. My dick jumps to attention when she runs her fingers by him once more, and I want grab them and put them right where I want them. Her body is cuddled into my side and her face is pressed against my pec.

"How long have I been out?" My voice is strained and when I look down at her, she looks up at me.

"Forty-eight hours." She wrinkles her nose at that, and I can't help but think it's a sexy look on her.

"I need to check on things out in the clubhouse." She doesn't say anything; she just sits up and waits for me to get out of bed. I'm still naked, and she's just wearing one of my tee shirts.

"Stav, I need some more clothes than what I have. I didn't exactly get to pack when Dex forced me to leave with him."

"You still have clothes in my dresser." She raises an eyebrow at me, but I ignore it and pull my body off my bed. I still feel like shit, but I need to get back to my men.

We both dress in silence, and when she's ready, she takes a seat on my bed and waits for me to finish pulling on my boots. Reaching for her hand, I help her up and end up almost falling on her instead. "Stav, you really should lay back down. The doc had to flush your system you had so much in you."

"Babe, I'll be fine." She frowns, but doesn't say anything else. She knows I don't back down when I have something set in my mind. I need to get out there and take control of my clubhouse. I need to see that Romeo took care of that stupid bitch Delilah, too.

Grabbing her hand, I lead her towards the bar. When the guys see me, they start making their way towards me. After over a dozen, 'glad to see you up and around's', I just want to find Romeo. I finally find him in the kitchen talking to Dex. "Go back into the bar. I'll be back in a minute." I whisper in Harlyn's ear. She looks between the guys before nodding her head, and making her way back through the door, letting it swing closed behind her. When I turn my attention back to my VP and SAA, I can see them checking me over.

"You should probably be on your back still, asshole." Romeo states.

"I'm not a fucking bitch, dickhead."

Dex starts to laugh and I give him a look that causes him to stop. He clears his throat and waits for me to say something useful. "What happened?" They both stare at me like I should remember, but I can't remember a damn thing but the yelling and someone putting their hands on me. I remember passing out in Harlyn's lap, but that's it.

"You disappeared for a while and I thought that you just went to your office. When Trix came back down, she said you were drinking Johnny the rest of the night, and I didn't think anything of it. Harlyn was acting all pouty and bitchy for a few hours and then left. We heard fighting in the hall, so we went over there, and Harlyn had Delilah on the floor beating the fuck out of her. You should see the damage she caused. I didn't know she was that fucking scrappy."

For the first time ever, I see that Romeo is in

awe of her. That's something that I've never seen from him. "Where is she?"

"Down in the garage. I thought that you'd like to talk to her before anything happened." Dex answers. Nodding my head, I motion for him to lead the way. We make our way out into the bar, and then towards the door, and we get stopped a few times as we go. I get a glimpse of Harlyn, but she has a frown on her face. I would bring her with me, but I already know how that went last time. Plus, I'm sure she won't like knowing what I'm about to do.

Once we get done with everyone's bitching and complaining, we make a beeline towards the garage. Romeo leads the way, and when we get inside, I see the mess Harlyn made of Delilah's face. Her eye is swollen, she has a fat lip, blood is matted in her blonde hair, and one of her cheekbones is swollen. Her eyes meet mine and they widen a fraction. This time she doesn't even open her mouth to say one word to me.

Before I can even ask her why she did it, I hear metal clang to the ground. When we turn, I see Harlyn standing there like a deer in the headlights. Instead of yelling at her to get out of here, I hold my arm up and she slowly starts to walk over to me. When she gets close enough, I wrap my hand around the back of her neck and pull her to me.

Her hands go to my chest and I stare into her eyes. The gasp behind us doesn't even bother me. I have Harlyn in my arms and that's all I can think of. Pulling her mouth up to mine, I kiss her deeply. Neither Dex, nor Romeo says anything, and they know I'm making a point to Delilah. When I break our kiss, I see the lust written all over Harlyn's face. She doesn't say anything, but she does look over in Delilah's direction.

When my eyes land on her, I see the anger in her eyes. She's always hated that I never got over Harlyn, but I never promised her, or any one of our whores, that I was anything more than a dick willing to fuck them once or twice. I was only out to get my dick wet, while Harlyn was out gallivanting the damn world.

"Why did you do it?" I turn my attention towards Delilah and she only stares at Harlyn.

"Because that stupid bitch comes strutting her little ass in here, and you forgot about the ones who been warming your bed since she left. She threw you to the curb like trash, Stavros, and you let the stupid bitch come right back into your arms." She shakes her head and laughs dryly. "You can't see anything but her whore ass. You let her fuck who knows how many men while she was away, and now you stick your dick inside of her again like she isn't some disease infested skank." She starts to laugh again and I feel Harlyn tense in my arms.

"You stupid bitch." Harlyn growls. She starts to move towards Delilah, but I wrap my arms around her waist and haul her back into my body.

"Stav." She snaps, turning around, pointing her finger into my chest. "She tried to rape you after drugging you. She deserves your wrath more than a lot of people. If you don't do something, I will." She grinds her teeth and I can see the fire burning in her eyes. "If it was some man who tried to do the same thing to me, you wouldn't even hesitate." She spits.

I look over at Romeo and Dex and they both shrug their shoulders. They both know she's right, and that it's exactly what I'd do. Hell, it's what I've done before. She knows this, they know this, and I know this. I didn't even think twice when I went after that fucker that had a knife to Harlyn's throat.

"God, Stavros, you're so pathetic. You're letting that bitch run your life and she only just came back." Before I can stop her this time, she goes charging at Delilah. I watch her fist go into her face and she knocks Delilah and her chair over, continuing to beat the fuck out of her.

After a few seconds, I haul Harlyn off of Delilah. She tries to fight me, but I whisper in her ear, "Stop." She stops fighting instantly, and she goes limp in my arms. "I'll deal with her. I want you to go back to the room and clean up. You're covered in blood." Her eyes meet mine, and they widen. Her breathing starts to ramp up, and she starts to hyperventilate.

"She okay?" Romeo asks.

Her legs give out and I pull her body to mine. I should have fuckin' sent her away. I knew better than this. Picking her up, I put one arm under her legs and the other behind her back. She wraps her arms around me. Burying her face in my chest, I feel the tears as they start to soak through my shirt. "I need to get her cleaned up. I'll be back." They both nod and I make my way out of the garage, and towards the clubhouse. People try to stop me when I walk in, but I ignore them, and push my way past everyone. Getting Harlyn into the room is my only concern right now.

Opening the door, I take her straight into the bathroom and start to strip her down. When she takes a look in the mirror, she goes ghost white and looks like she might pass out. In all the years I've known her, she's never been one to instigate a fight, and I've sure as hell never seen her beat the fuck out of another bitch.

"Where did you learn to fight from?" Her eyes meet mine and I can't really read her expression.

"I don't know. I didn't think I was capable of that." She looks down at her hands and more tears start to fall down her face. For the first time, I don't know how to help her. I don't know what to do to make things okay for her. She looks heartbroken and in shock with the amount of damage she did.

"What happens next?" Her voice is awfully low and I'm afraid of her freaking out even more than she just was.

"She isn't going to live. She drugged me. Fuck, she even tried to fuck me while I was drugged. There is no way in hell I would have touched her otherwise, and she's going to pay for that." She swallows loudly and she looks like she's going to be sick.

She runs to the toilet and pukes. Grabbing her hair, I keep it out of her face until she finishes emptying her stomach. She sits on the floor and just looks at her hands. I need to get her in the shower now.

Chapter Nine

Starting the shower, I watch Harlyn carefully. She looks like she's ready to bolt, but I'm not going to let her. She has no idea what it's like to kill someone. I'm sure if I didn't pull her off of Delilah, she would have. Stripping down, I pull her off the ground, and force her into the shower with me. The warm water doesn't even snap her out of her thoughts.

Harlyn is in a sort of comatose state. She doesn't say anything and she doesn't move. I take my time washing her body, her hands and her hair. Her eyes are puffy and red from the tears she cried, but other than that, you could barely tell anything was wrong with her.

Grabbing one of her hands, I make sure I got all the blood off of her before doing the same to the next one. When she's completely clean, I wash my body and hair before I shut the water off and help her out. I grab the towel off the counter and quickly dry us both off. Picking her up, I take her to the bed and lay us both down.

"Stav." Her broken whisper fills my ears and I can hear how upset she is.

"Yeah, baby?"

"I don't want to be like you." I flinch at her words, but the truth is, I don't want her to be like me either. I want her to stay the pure woman I fell in love with. All my darkness will do is swallow her whole, and spit her back out just as damaged as me. I killed my first man at twelve, and although I would do it again, I don't want a life like that for her.

She deserves better, and I will fight like hell to make sure she never has to do what I did to survive. I didn't have a choice though, but I will make sure she always has a choice.

Harlyn curls her body into mine, and all thoughts of killing Delilah are gone. I just hold her. Nothing separating our bodies, just like we've spent so many nights in this room. Where I spent so many nights of being able to show her the real me that is hidden under the monster inside of my chest, the one that claws its way out when anyone I care about is being threatened or hurt.

She doesn't say anything for hours, and I know

that I need to get back to Dex and Romeo, but I can't leave her alone while she's like this. She didn't leave my side after I was drugged, so I won't leave her either.

When Harlyn finally falls asleep a few hours later, I slip out of the bed and pull on my jeans from the bathroom. They are just going to get bloody anyway, so why put on a clean pair. After getting dressed, I kiss her forehead. She looks peaceful, finally, and I want it to stay that way. Slipping out of the room quietly, I make my way towards the garage.

Walking through the clubhouse, it's eerily quiet. No one is up and around since we're on lockdown. I'm just waiting for all the damn drama to start around here. Opening the door of the garage, I see Delilah sitting upright in the chair again, her head is hanging down in an awkward position.

"Bout time." Romeo says, hidden in the corner of the room.

"She finally just fell asleep. She's a fucking wreck." He shakes his head, but he doesn't say anything else.

"Let's get this shit dealt with so I can get back to her before she wakes up." He smirks at that and we both make our way towards Delilah. I've never killed a bitch before. I've never had a reason to, but she did something I can't overlook.

Kicking the chair, she startles awake. I thought

she looked bad before, but now she looks even worse. Harlyn really did a number on her. Almost every inch of her face is bruised and swollen. You can barely tell who she is anymore. "Why did you do it?"

She tries to spit blood at me, but she misses. Walking closer, I grab her by the neck and start to squeeze. She starts to gasp for breath, but she can't move her hands to try and get me to stop. When I release her throat, she starts to cough and gasp for air. "If you don't fucking tell me, I'll keep doing this all night. I won't let you die. I'll just keep torturing you until you give me the information I want."

When she doesn't say anything, I reach forward and grab her neck again. My fingers flex around her neck, and I almost don't let go in time to watch her cough and gasp for air again. She doesn't know that I don't give a fuck why she did it, I only care that Harlyn is in my bed, and freaked the fuck out about what she did to Delilah. I'm doing this for Harlyn.

Before I can grab her neck again, she finally gives me the answer I was looking for. "Flint." She coughs up some blood and then continues to speak. "He paid me to drug that stupid whore of yours and get her out of the building so he could take her. Instead, I put it in your bottle in the drawer..." she trails off and her head falls forward. She's losing consciousness. Luckily I have all the information I need.

Grabbing my knife, I thrust it into her chest and

her eyes meet mine as I watch the life drain out of them. Her head lolls to the side and she looks like she's staring right at Romeo.

Pulling my knife out of her chest, I wipe the blade on my jeans and put it back in the holder strapped to my body. "You think he really sent her in here to get Harlyn out?"

"I don't give a fuck. I'll kill the bastard. He declared war when he openly threatened Harlyn, and I ain't backin' down."

"In his trying to get her, he let some dumb bitch try and lure her out, instead, she drugged your ass. You were so fucking high on whatever shit she gave you that your heart stopped for a second. If she would have given that to Harlyn, she would have died." I nod, but my brain is running in a million different directions.

I want to go and fucking gut the bastard, but I also have to be smart about it. My need for revenge is almost winning the battle in my head. "Get the prospects to take her and leave her on their doorstep. They wanted a fucking war, they'll get one. I'll burn down every fucking building they own until I take every last one of the fuckers out."

Stalking off, I have to clear my head before I go to see Harlyn, but I can't bring myself to. Instead, I make my way to my room and as soon as I open the door, I see her sitting up with the covers to her chest.

Anger flares up in me as I think about what Romeo said. If Delilah would have drugged her, she would have died. Her body is a third the size of mine.

Her eyes scan over my body and I know that she can see the blood on me. I watch as she crawls out from under the blanket and starts to make her way towards me. Something inside me snaps, and before I can stop myself from moving, I grab her by the throat and push her back on the bed. Her eyes widen for a second before she reaches up to touch my face.

No words are said but I can feel my heart pounding in my chest and the need to fuck her is burning in my stomach. I'm a bastard, this much I know. Instead of pulling away from her, I slam my mouth down on hers and kiss her like I'm fuckin' starving. In a way I am, but it's not fair to her.

Her body reacts to mine and I run my free hand down her chest and pinch her nipple. Grinding my jean cover dick into her bare pussy builds a fire inside of me, and I need to get inside of her right now. I release her nipple and suck the other in my mouth as I undo my jeans and start to move them down my hips. Her moans fill the room as I bite her nipple. Her body arches up into me, and I squeeze a little tighter on her neck.

Kicking off my boots and jeans, I slide between her thighs again and I slam into her - hard. Part of me doesn't even care if I hurt her right now, and the other part of me wants to take my time - make love to her beautiful body, treat her like the goddess she is. Every thrust into her pussy is hard and deep, causing her to close her eyes. Her hands go to my hips and she starts to move them up my body, pulling my shirt up with them. Releasing her throat, I pull my shirt off and toss it behind me on the floor.

Reaching down to her pussy, I rub her clit roughly and I feel her whole body start to tense around me. She needs the frenzied fuck just as much as I do. Flipping us over, I get her on top of me, and she starts to slide up and down my dick fast and hard, bottoming out on me every time. Her hands run up her body and she pinches both of her nipples in between her index fingers and thumbs.

Just watching her do this gets my dick harder than it was a few seconds ago.

Thrusting up to meet her pussy, I force her down on me hard. My hands grip her ass as I move her. I release one ass cheek to give her ass a hard smack. Her head falls back and she moans out my name. Harlyn rides me hard and fast, and I keep smacking her ass until I feel her pussy tighten, and she groans out her release. Flipping her back over, I pound into her harder, and grip her throat once more. She cries out, but I don't stop. I can't stop. The darkness clouds my vision and I lean forward to take her nipple into my mouth again. Everything else fades away and I don't even realize what I'm doing anymore. I can't control my own body.

When I come inside of her, I thrust a few more times before I collapse on top of her. She doesn't try and push me off of her; she just runs her hands through my hair and down my back until I can move again. When the darkness clears, I slowly pull out of her and roll over to my back. I watch her from the corner of my eye, and I see her look down at her chest before she moves to straddle my hips.

My eyes catch the marks I just left on her skin. She doesn't say anything; she just looks into my eyes. Reaching up, I run my finger over the mark on her left nipple. Our eyes meet, and it's almost like I can feel everything she's thinking in this exact moment.

My attention moves to her neck, and I see my fingerprints. Closing my eyes, I feel the regret. I never want to hurt her. Moving out from under her, I watch her fall off the bed, but I don't even try to help her. Instead, I get up and feel my anger lash out. Putting my hand through the wall takes a little of the anger out from deep inside of me, but it's not enough to get me to calm down.

Her small hand lands on my back and I spin around. I've always tried like hell to keep her from seeing me like this, but it was never able to happen. She knows how this shit builds in me, and I hate that it's her skin that I'm leaving marks on. It's only happened once, and after that, she didn't stick around for long. After we brought her back from being kidnapped I left marks on her skin just like this, I couldn't stop myself then either. I already knew my days with her again were numbered, but I was hoping that she would change her mind and stay with me.

My breathing is ragged, but she doesn't let that stop her from walking closer to me. When she goes to touch me again, I grab her wrist and stop her. If I don't stop her, I will probably leave another mark on her silky smooth skin. "Don't." I growl. Her hand shrinks back and then her eyebrows furrow together.

She starts to make her way closer to me and there is nothing that I can do to stop her. "I won't let you slowly destroy yourself and me." Her voice comes out stronger than I thought it would. She reaches out again and this time I let her touch me. "Stav, let me help you." She presses both of her palms against my stomach and I look down at her.

Her eyes are full of determination and she doesn't look scared of me. My eyes scan over her body again, and the only things I can see are the marks that are now marring her skin. I am the reason she ran a year and a half ago, and I'll be that same reason she runs when the lockdown is lifted. Why can't I just stay away from her? All I do is fuck shit up between us.

Feeling her hands on me starts to push the darkness back. She stands on her tip toes, and she's still a few inches too short. She moves her hands up to my neck and pulls my head down so she can reach. "I won't run out on you this time. You need me." She ghosts her lips over mine and I don't know whether or not I should wrap my arms around her. I don't know what she wants, or what she's going to do the next time I can't control it.

Harlyn wraps her arms around my neck and I pull her body into mine. Her body fits mine perfectly still. Her softer curves press against the hard planes of my body. Spending hours in the gym was the only way I was able to keep semi sane after she left. Closing my eyes, I breathe in her scent and memorize it. Losing her will be my downfall, and I hope that day never comes. I would rather fall on my own knife than lose my only saving grace.

Chapter Ten

After seeing her with the marks that I left on her body, we spent the rest of the night in bed. My eyes could only focus on the marks that I left, but she didn't want to talk about it. Instead, she forced me to tell her what happened with Delilah. She knew that it was the reason behind me putting my hands on her. I used her body, and I shouldn't have.

"What's it like?" her question brings me out of the trance I put myself in. my hand tightens on her hip, and I look down at her face that is now resting on my chest.

"What?" I play dumb because I don't know exactly how to explain it to her, or hell, even to myself.

"After you did what you did in the garage to Delilah, or even after you killed that man in front of me, you go from the man I love to something else. What is that like?" her fingers move in circles around my stomach, so I try to focus on that instead of the question. "Please Stav. I really want to be able to understand you. I want to help you."

Hearing the sad tone in her voice, I give in and give her the answer she's wanting. "It's not something I can control. I feel like something is trying to claw its way out of my chest. Everything disappears, and I'm not even aware of what I'm doing. Sometimes I feel like I'm suffocating until it happens." I sit up, forcing her to move, too. Her head goes into my lap and I lay back against the headboard. Running my fingers through her hair, I watch the look in her eyes as I talk.

"After everything happened with that bastard who kidnapped you, I hated what I became. I never wanted to hurt you. Harlyn, I'm sorry." She bites her lip and I lean forward to press my lips against hers. "The anger that consumed me after I gutted him with my knife, took over every aspect of me. I couldn't stop after the knife dug into him the first time. All the built up rage from over the years became the only thing I could think about."

"Was that the first time?" Her eyes are almost pleading for me to say yes, but I know that it isn't. Tonight won't be the last time either.

"No. It doesn't happen a lot. The first time was when I was twelve." I hang my head in shame. I can't even bring myself to look at her. For the first time ever, I'm ashamed of who I am. She deserves better than this.

"What happened?" I look at her and I don't see any judgement in her eyes, so I decide to tell her why I killed someone at that age.

"My father died when I was really young, maybe two or three. My mom raised me and my brother the best she could. One day we came home from school early, and we found her laying on the floor bleeding while the bastard she was dating was kicking the shit out of her. I didn't think, I just acted. I wasn't a big kid, but I had some strength. So I tackled him and just started to pound on him until my little brother pulled me off of him." Her hand grips mine and it gives me the strength to keep speaking.

"He wasn't breathing, and my mom freaked out because she thought that if anyone found out, they would send me away. Instead of telling the cops, she called my uncle, my dad's brother. Viktor came to the house and he made it all go away. He didn't question what happened. He just made sure that we were protected. I didn't learn until I got older what he actually did. When I was eighteen, he approached me to join his organization, but I declined. He wanted to use me as a trained killer."

"You only kill to protect the ones you love." Her voice is whisper soft, and, in a way, it makes me feel better about what I've done over the years.

"My brother ended up saying yes to his offer, and I haven't spoken to him since." She moves to straddle my lap and she pulls my face into her chest. Breathing in her scent, I just let her hold me. I never knew it was possible to have someone as fucking perfect and pure as Harlyn.

"You couldn't have stopped him. He made his own decision, and you made yours." Looking up at her, I can see that she means the words she just spoke.

"Yeah but we are the same person. I kill people, and so does he."

She pulls away, and grabs my chin like I've done to her a number of times before. "No, you listen to me. You are protecting the people you love. He is killing because he's being told to. There is nothing the same about that. Stav, you are so much more than you give yourself credit for. You're not the bad man you think you are. Yeah, I don't agree with you on the whole killing people thing, but I also know that you don't go around doing it to make someone else happy. You don't take orders from anyone."

Looking into her eyes, I can see how much she wants to believe the words. "Harlyn, I'm just as bad as they are. I may not kill to get ahead in life, or to take over something, but I do kill. Shit, I can't even promise that I won't kill again. I can only promise you that I will never intentionally hurt you." I reach my hand up and cup her cheek.

"I know I've hurt you more than once already, but if I'm being honest, you're the only person who can calm me down when I'm like that. You save me from myself." She leans into my touch, and I wrap my arms around her body, pulling her closer to me. I'm prepared for her to pull away, but she doesn't. Instead, she wraps her arms around my neck.

"I love you Stav. That will never change. Sometimes, you just scare the crap out of me. I'm tired of running from you when I should be running to you. You're the only man to ever give a damn about me, and to treat me like a princess." Her lips cascade down onto mine and she kisses me softly.

"You took your time with me. You made sure that I was really ready before you took my virginity, and you have never made me feel like I wasn't good enough. Just promise me you won't tell me when it happens again." Her eyes are boring into my soul, and I want to promise her everything and more, but I can't control it when it happens.

"I will probably find you after it happens. I'll need to be able to get the darkness out of me, and you're the only one who takes it from me. Your touch, your body - it's the only way I've been able to come back from it." Her hand goes to my chest and she puts her fingers over my rapidly beating heart.

"Then let me help you. Just don't give me the details." I swear, I don't think I heard her right. She can't knowingly want to help me. I'm too much of a bastard for her to want anything to do with me.

"I can't hurt you again." I breathe. My eyes are on hers, and she never looks away or changes her expression.

"You won't. I trust you." She leans forward and presses her lips to mine again. We don't say anything; we just speak with our mouths. She runs her tongue down my neck, and I groan out. Before she can go any further, someone bangs on the door.

"Prez. We need you out here." She sighs against my chest, and places one more kiss to my skin before she pulls away.

"I'll be back." I kiss her nose, and she nods her head. She scoots off my lap and gets under the covers. Looking over my shoulder at her, I can see the acceptance and love written all over her. Maybe if I would have just told her this shit from the beginning, we wouldn't have been apart all that time. "I love you Harlyn." She grins at my words and I can't help but smile back at her.

After I get dressed, I pull on my boots and make my way out into the other room. When I come around the corner, I see a brick laying on the ground by one of the windows by the front door. Walking over to it, I pick it up and read the message.

An eye for an eye. A woman for a woman. Can't wait until the day comes that I get to taste her. Does she scream out as you fuck her? I bet she does. I'll ruin her for you. She will never be the same after I've had my fill of her.

"When did this happen?" I grate out. I can see fucking red, and I want to go find this bastard and gut him for even thinking about putting his hands on her.

"Just heard it a few minutes before I came and got you." Romeo states. He looks around the room and then motions towards one of the prospects that is supposed to be on guard.

"Where were you when this shit happened?" I grab him by the collar and watch him. His eyes widen but he doesn't say a word. "Where the fuck were you?" I demand.

"I... I... I... was taking a piss. I heard the glass break and came running back in." I release my hold on him and he starts to fumble back. He rights himself before he falls to the ground.

Looking over at Romeo, I nod my head and he grabs his phone out of his pocket. "Tell the men, church first thing. I want to kill those fucking bastards. I don't give a shit what anyone has planned. They better fucking be there first thing." Turning towards the prospect, I give him an order before walking back to my room. "Clean this shit up and cover the window." He nods and scurries off to find what he needs.

Making my way back into my room, I see that Harlyn is staring at me. Stripping out of my clothes, I make my way towards the shower to wash away any remaining blood on my body. She doesn't deserve to have the blood on my hands touch her. I should have done this earlier, but I couldn't. All I could think of was getting inside of her.

As I stand in silence letting the hot water melt the remainder of Delilah from my skin, I hang my head in shame. Harlyn doesn't deserve me or my demons. All she deserves is the best, and I will never be that for her. I'll be able to protect her and love her more than any other mother fucker, but that's it.

I stay under the shower head until I'm scrubbed raw and the water has gone cold. Nothing can erase the blood that stains me, but at least I know that she is protected. Shutting the water off, I dry off and toss the wet towel over the curtain rod. Making my way out into the room, I see her curled up on my side of the bed.

Turning the light in the bathroom off, I watch the room turn dark, and I make my way over to the bed. Sliding under the covers, I curl up into her body, and she moves just enough for me to lay right beside her. She doesn't open her eyes, and I can't help but stare at her. It reminds me of the night I took her virginity.

"Stav." She whines, backing away from me. My hand grazed over the tattoo that she just got. Seeing my name on her wrist gets me fucking harder than I've ever been. I want to plow into her right now, but I know I'll hurt her.

"Harlyn come here." I demand. She sits up and crawls over to me. She gets closer, so I wrap my arm around her and pull her body against mine. "Baby you're going to forget all about the pain in your wrist when my dick slides inside of that pussy of mine." She gives me a small smirk and wraps her arms around my neck, careful to not put her wrist against me.

"What are you waiting for?" she bites her bottom lip.

Pushing her back on the bed, I lay on top of her and kiss her mouth. Slowly taking it further, I slip my tongue between her lips, and run my hands down her body until I come to the bottom of her dress. I slide her dress up until I get to her panties. My fingers brush against her pussy, and I can feel her arousal through the silk thong. Sliding it down her ass and legs, I pull it off and toss it on the ground. I sit us both up so I can pull her dress up and over her head. She has no bra on and I take one of her nipples into my mouth as I slowly start to work my finger into her wet heat.

Every thrust of my finger brings moans out of her perfect lips. Never have I had a woman who was so sensitive to my touch. When I add a second finger, she arches her back into the air. "Oh God." She moans. I work her up quickly, and I feel her pussy clamp down around my fingers as she comes. Her eyes roll into the back of her head as she screams out my name.

While she comes down from her orgasm, I get off the bed and start to undress. When she finally opens her eyes and looks up at me, I can see the satisfaction written all over her face. For the last few month's I've been getting her ready to take me inside of her. If her parents knew where she was going at night, they would ground her for the rest of her life.

Sliding back up the bed, I tower over her and kiss my way up her body. Resting between her thighs, I can feel how wet she still is. "I don't want to hurt you, baby." I whisper against her skin.

"I want you." I can hear the need in her voice and I want to slam inside of her, but I know it would hurt her. Instead, I slowly enter her, going inch by inch until I come into contact with her hymen.

"It's gonna hurt babe." I whisper. She nods her head and bites her lip. When her feet urge me to go again, I thrust the rest of the way inside of her and I hear her cry out in pain. Dropping my head to her chest, I try not to move.

"Stav, move please." I look up at her and give her a questioning look. "I'm okay. I promise." Nodding my head, I start to move again and I can feel her pussy taking me in more easily and before long, we are both coming. Pulling out of her, I cuddle into her body, and she puts her head against my chest.

"Amazing." She whispers out of breath.

"I have a feeling that every time with you is going to be amazing." I press a kiss to the side of her head and we both fall asleep.

Chapter Eleven

Waking up, I don't feel her warmth. Opening my eyes, I look around the room and don't see any sign of her. Did she leave? Jumping out of bed, I pull on a pair of jeans and make my way to the bathroom. When I don't see her, I pull on my boots and a shirt. Walking out of the room, I search the hallway and the bar area, but don't see anyone. I hear some giggles coming from the kitchen and when I open the door, I see Harlyn and Trix making breakfast.

Silently letting out the breath I was holding, I make my way over to Harlyn and pull her body back into mine. She squeals in surprise and I see the grin on Trix's face. "I missed you this morning." I whisper in her ear. I bite her ear lobe and she starts to giggle again.

"We wanted to make everyone breakfast." She finally gets out. I look over at Trix, and she gives me a knowing look. Her smile isn't as bright as it normally is, but I have a feeling that it has something to do with not being able to show any emotion towards E. She loves him, and he's too afraid of what that bitch he's married to will do when she finds out.

"Where's the little man?" I ask looking around the room.

"He's in my room still asleep." She says shyly. Walking over to her, I pull her in for a hug and whisper in her ear.

"I'll watch him until you girls are done." She pulls away and looks into my eyes for a second before she agrees.

I give Harlyn one more kiss before I go to get Blade. When I make my way towards the room we gave Trix, I can't help but think about Harlyn having my baby. I don't even know why I would think about it, but deep down inside it makes me happy. I know I'm not father material, but having another little piece of heaven in this fucked up world I live in, would make things worth fighting for even more than before.

Opening the door, I see E standing there watching Blade sleep. Closing the door behind me, I wait for him to turn around and look at me before I say anything. "Prez, I know I shouldn't be in here, but I had to see him." Walking closer to my brother, I put a hand on his shoulder and watch Blade with him.

He's a mini E, and there is no way that he would be able to deny that that little boy is his. Every feature of Blade's is from him. He looks nothing like Trix.

"Does she know?" I ask.

"That I sneak in here? No, she'd be pissed. I fucked this shit up so damn bad. I want to be part of his life." He runs his hands over his face, and I get it. If I were in the same position as him, I would be angry with myself. "Tina is starting to put it together. I can only imagine what she's going to say when she sees him closer up. Trix has stayed as far away from us as she can since she got here. Not that I blame her."

"Why aren't you giving her money?" My voice is controlled even though I would love nothing more than to rip into him. I get that he doesn't want his wife to know about Blade, but he still has a responsibility to that little boy.

He closes his eyes and shakes his head. "For the longest time I didn't want to believe that he was mine. Trix sleeps with all the brothers." I don't let him keep going because he'll just piss me off.

"She hasn't slept with any of the brothers in the last year. I told her it was her choice when she came to me. She wanted out of the game, and I give her a job working at one of the clubs at a waitress. That way she was making money and being able to provide for herself." He turns towards me, and I see the shocked look on his face.

"She only came around for me?" I shrug my shoulders. Shit, I don't know.

"I only know that she wanted to make a change in her life, and I gave her the opportunity. I could tell she was in love with someone, just didn't know who until she showed up pregnant and alone. You broke her when you said you didn't want anything to do with her after she got pregnant. Probably because you thought you weren't the father, but brother there is no denying that little boy is yours." He nods, but doesn't say anything.

"Yet you still called her when you wanted your dick sucked, or a fuck. She isn't your damn play thing. You will be providing for Blade. I don't give a fuck what happens in your marriage because of this. Man the fuck up, and take care of your kid."

He nods and looks back at the bed where Blade is still asleep. "I will Prez."

"I gave her money the other day. She's working her ass off and doesn't have a pot to piss in." Before I can say anything else, he surprises me.

"Take what you gave her out of my cut. Every time. I want to take care of them." I nod my head and I see Blade's eyes open and he reaches out for me. Walking over to the bed, I pick him up. He rests his head against my shoulder and stares at his father.

A little hand reaches out towards E, and he almost looks unsure of what to do. I move closer towards him and he tentatively reaches out and grabs Blade's chubby little hand. Blade looks up at him and watches his every move. The door flies open and I watch as Tina comes barging in. E looks pissed and I can't help but shake my head. "You're fucking that whore aren't you? Where is she?" She goes to look around the room, but E grabs her and pulls her back towards the door.

"Shut the fuck up." He growls. She tries to fight him and I feel Blade's little body start to tense up. When he starts to cry, Tina stops her struggling and looks over at me and Blade.

"You son of a bitch," she hisses. She tries to get out of his arms to get closer to Blade and I, but E never lets her go. He pulls her out of the room, and I take Blade towards the kitchen to his mom. When I get there, she comes rushing over to us.

"What happened?" She looks nervous as she takes him from me.

"Tina knows." I reply. I hear that bitch screaming out in the bar area, and it keeps getting louder.

Looking behind the girls, I see all the food that's ready, and Trix starts to make her way out into the bar with Blade. Grabbing Harlyn's hand, I drag her out of the kitchen. When we all stop in front of where Tina is still struggling to get away from E, she turns her anger on Trix. She points at Trix and starts screaming at her. "You stupid slut! I will make sure you regret ever touching my old man! That kid is never going to know his father. I'll make sure of it!"

Trix holds her head up high and doesn't let the words Tina is spitting affect her. "Get your fucking ol' lady on a leash E. I won't have that type of disrespect in front of a child." I demand. Tina shrinks back, but I don't give a fuck. I hope that bitch does us all a favor and jumps off a damn bridge. She does nothing but fuck with E and make his life miserable.

I'm glad that stupid bitch is afraid of me. She won't like what I fucking do if she even thinks about hurting one hair on either Blade's, or Trix's head. They are like family, and I won't think twice about making an example out of her.

E finally drags her ass out of my bar, and Harlyn goes over to Trix and wraps her arms around both of them. They whisper to each other and more people start to make their way out of the hallways and towards the middle of the room. When Trix isn't shaking any more, she brings Blade back over to me. "I got him." I kiss her forehead, and she nods before following Harlyn into the kitchen. Before the kitchen door closes, Harlyn gives me a wink and disappears just like Trix did.

"Prospects. Get some tables and chairs set up. The girls made breakfast." All four prospects go to the storage and start to set everything up. When the first of the dishes come out, the girls set them out on the bar. A few of the other women follow them back and start to help bring out the rest of the plates for them. Paper plates, napkins, and utensils are also brought out, and the kids get their plates first.

When everything is set out, Harlyn comes back over to me and wraps her arm around my waist. Kissing the top of her head, I watch as Blade tries to grab her hair and pull on it. She grabs his little hand and kisses it. She releases me and takes him from me.

Watching her with Blade brings an ache into my chest. I want to give her that so damn bad. I think I want it more for myself than anything else. Watching everyone sitting down eating as a family makes me proud, but I still don't have a family of my own.

"Stav." She whispers.

"Yeah?" I ask watching her.

"Have you ever thought of having your own?" She doesn't say any more than that, and I grin. Pulling her to me, I kiss the side of her head.

"Only if it was with you." I smirk at her and she grins. "What do you think about that?" She stares at me trying to search my face for something, but I can't tell if she finds what she is looking for or not.

"Why only with me?" her voice is low and she

looks around the room at everyone eating before she turns her attention back to me.

"Because you're the only woman I want. The only one I would ever consider having kids with." She gives me a questioning look, but I don't bother answering her. Leading her towards bar to grab us both food, I see Trix coming towards us with a bottle for Blade. She takes him from her and goes to sit on the couch with him.

Harlyn makes Trix a plate first and then walks it over to her before coming back to me to help me with ours. "Is E's ol' lady going to cause another scene?"

"Don't know, baby. I sure hope she keeps her mouth shut. I don't want to have to deal with her. I already warned all my men that they need to keep their ol' ladies on a leash while we are all here under one roof. I don't stand for this shit." She nods her head and puts some eggs and bacon on my plate before reaching for the spoon in the fruit bowl.

When she's done loading our plates full of food, I lead her towards one of the tables that doesn't have anyone sitting at it. I set the plates down, and then pull out her chair and help her in. "This reminds me more of the days before." She muses. I wasn't always a jackass, I used to be a better man for her. I did everything in my power to make sure she was loved and protected. Now, I don't know how to balance it like I did before. One wrong move and I'm sure I'll be scaring her off again.

Taking my seat, I watch her eat for a second and the small little moans she makes when she tastes something she likes. "This is so good." She says pointing at something on her plate. I can't even focus on that, all I can do is watch as her eyes close as she moans in appreciation again.

"You keep moaning like that and I'll be taking your sweet cunt right now in front of everyone." Her eyes open wide, and she gives me a devious little grin. She goes back to eating, and every other bite has a moan attached to it. I have to bite my cheek to keep my ass in my own chair. Eating quickly, I continue to watch her. When she bites her lip, I can't help but unzip my jeans and then pull her sexy ass into my lap.

I slide her dress up and over her ass, while she turns to look back at me. I raise an eyebrow at her and she grins at me. She stands up enough for me to line myself up with her pussy and she sits back down, taking me inside of her sweet cunt. I groan at the feeling as she starts to rock on me.

Going back to eating, I have one hand on her hip, controlling how fast she goes, and when she stops. I work her up a few times and she huffs out when I don't let her come. She continues to eat small bites, and I do the same. When my VP comes over to us, she stops moving completely.

"Prez, when are we doing church?" He asks.

"Give me a few more minutes and we can gather them all." Harlyn looks back at me, and I place a kiss on her shoulder.

He nods his head and makes his way over towards the men and starts to let them know about church. I start to move Harlyn again, and this time when I work her up, I don't stop her from coming. Her hands brace the table, and I hear her quiet moans. Her pussy tightens around me, and my balls tighten as I spill my cum inside of her. She slowly keeps moving, riding my orgasm out.

chapter Twelve

Once I got Harlyn off my dick, I tucked myself back into my jeans and tugged her dress back down her ass. She had taken our plates back to the kitchen and was now walking back towards me with a satisfied grin on her face.

My fingers flit over her neck and I see where she covered the bruise on her neck. It still fucking kills me that I put those marks on her skin. "Don't." She warns. I go to say something, but I can't get the words out. Instead, I lean down and capture her mouth with mine, kissing her deeply. Her arms wrap around my waist and she stands on her tiptoes to give me more.

Pulling away from her before I'm ready, I kiss her once more, and make my way towards church.

Once all my men are seated, I take my seat and

slam the gavel on the table. "So I brought you all into church this morning because last night we got a threat against Harlyn. Someone threw a brick through one of windows and left a note for me. It read "An eye for an eye. A woman for a woman. Can't wait until the day comes that I get to taste her. Does she scream out as you fuck her? I bet she does. I'll ruin her for you. She will never be the same after I've had my fill of her." I look around the room at all of my men and see the anger written all over their faces.

"I want this fucker dealt with. I don't want another replay of what happened a year and a half ago. I won't let anything else happen to my ol' lady." They nod their heads. Through the brief silence of our meeting, we hear screaming. E is the first one out of his chair, and he's out the door before I can even say anything. Jumping up, I rush out of the church doors, and see Tina running right towards Trix. Before she can get to her, E grabs Tina and pushes her into the wall. Trix is standing with Blade on her hip watching the whole scene play out before her. Tina is damn fucking lucky that E caught her before she touched that little boy.

"Bitch, I will fucking kill you if you hurt either of them," E growls at Tina. Her eyes widen and she tries to push him off of her, but he doesn't move. Looking over at Trix, I see Harlyn standing with her. Making my way towards them, I stop and look them both over before I ask them anything.

"What happened?" I demand. Harlyn moves

towards me and looks me in the eye.

"She started screaming at Trix saying that she's a whore and a bitch. She swore that by the end of things, she would be the one raising Elec's son." My eyes find E's, and I know he heard what she just said.

"You okay Trix?" I ask. She nods her head slightly and looks down at Blade.

"Yeah, he's just a little shook up. We'll be fine." She whispers. She keeps watching the way E is talking to his ol' lady in hushed tones. Every now and then she gives Trix a dirty look, but E forces her attention back on him.

E pushes her against the wall again and reiterates his point. "Don't fucking touch either of them. She's always going to be the mother of my son. I don't give a fuck if you don't like it or not. It happened and I will be part of his life." I hear Trix gasp and when I turn to look at her, I see the tears welling in her eyes. She doesn't say anything, she just keeps quiet.

"Har, take her to her room until we are done. I don't want any more shit." She nods her head and grabs Trix's hand and drags her towards the rooms. Watching them go, I can't help but be proud of how far we've come since she came back a few days ago.

As soon as E lets Tina go, he makes his way back towards me and comes to a stop. "Are they okay?" Slapping him on the back, I turn and lead him back towards the door where everyone has gathered.

"Yeah, a little shaken up, but fine. You need to get a fuckin' handle on your bullshit. We're all stuck in this damn place together, and I won't let this shit keep happening."

"I got you Prez. I didn't expect this shit to happen." I push him inside the room and pull the door closed behind me. Everyone gets back to their chairs and I sit back down.

"Back to business. I want to up security. I have a feeling that they are going to attack us sooner than expected." A few members grunt out in response, and the others just nod. "I want to make sure that everyone in the family is protected, not just Harlyn and Melissa."

"Keep your eyes peeled and let me know if you see anything else strange. I want to get a group to do some leg work on getting intel, and another spying on them. I want to know their weaknesses, and I want the information now." I demand, hitting my hand on the table.

I want to get these fuckers before they get any of us. Banging the gavel on the table, I watch my men all disburse back into the bar, and I follow behind them. On my way out of church, I call for the prospects to clean up the mess from breakfast. Once they start working, I make my way back to my office. I have some paperwork I need to get caught up on, and now that everything is quiet, it's the perfect time to do it.

Closing the door to my office, I walk behind my desk and take a seat. After going over the profit loss sheet for our bar, I think back to when Harlyn wanted to play bartender for me. She dropped six bottles of liquor on the ground, and every drink was way too fucking sweet. She giggled every time I made a face when I was testing it, and I ended up fucking her on top of the bar.

Shaking the memories from my head, I hear my phone go off in my pocket. When I pull it out, I see a buddy of mine's number on the screen. "Hey Trent." I answer. Pushing away from my desk, I put my feet on top and lean back in my chair.

"Hey man. Not sure if you knew, but word on the street is that someone is looking for your ol' lady."

"What information did you get?" I question.

"From what I've been told, they are going to strike when you least expect it. Flint is going to make you wish you never let his ol' lady into your clubhouse. He said that he's going to take his time with her and then gut her like you gutted the last man who touched her."

I feel my body go cold at the words of my friend. "You sure?" I ask quietly. I can feel the monster wanting to tear through me and go after him, but I keep picturing Harlyn's face. Knowing that she's safe and sound in my room, for now, is keeping the monster inside of me at bay.

"Yeah, as sure as I can be. He wants to show every other club what he's capable of, and for some reason, he's after you. I don't get what he wants with your ol' lady if you aren't even together anymore." Shaking my head, I try and focus on the words he's saying.

"She's back here with me. I sent my sergeant at arms to Vegas and had him bring her back when I first got wind of what Flint was planning. Maybe next time he'll get fucking smart, and not tell everyone and their god damn mothers about his plan."

"So she's safe?" He asks.

"Yeah. No one will get their hands on her while she's here with me." I state. I know what he's going to ask next, and it's only because I called him and begged him to help me find her last time. Trent can find out almost any fuckin' thing, and he's loyal as fuck. He's never let me down before, and I know he won't now.

"What if you let your guard down again, and someone grabs her off the streets? Or what about Slick's ol' lady?" I know he's trying to get a reaction out of me, but I won't give him one.

"That won't happen. We're on lockdown right now and no one is going out alone, especially those two." My jaw is tight as I speak through clenched teeth.

"Shit happens, brother. I'll see if I can get anything else. I will call if I find anything new." I don't even bother saying anything back to him as I hit the end button and toss my phone on the desk.

My mind starts to think of all the different possibilities, and a knock at my door brings my attention back to what I need to focus on. "Come in." I yell out. The door opens and I see Romeo come in. He takes a seat across from me, and puts an ankle over his knee.

"You get any info from Trent?"

"Not anything we didn't already know. Just that he'd strike when we least expected it, and that he was going to gut her like I gutted the last man who touched her." Just thinking about what I did to the first motherfucker that touched Harlyn after she left me makes my chest ache. I can't stop myself from remembering the way I felt after I watched the life seep out of his body.

It's been six long fuckin' months since Harlyn walked away from me. I never meant to hurt her, and I would give anything to have her back in my arms. As soon as I got the call from Cash, I couldn't stop myself from getting on my bike and making my way to where she is now. Romeo didn't trust to me go alone, so of course, like the big brother he acts like, he followed me. He tried to talk me off the ledge, but there was nothing that could have been said, or done, to make me think twice about what I was going to do.

We staked out her apartment and the minute I saw the fucker, I wanted to go after him, but she was standing in the door way. She looked at him almost the same way she looked at me. She had the same look in her eyes after I spent hours worshipping her body. He turned and said goodbye to her with a dopey grin on his face and I wanted to gut him then and there. Every ounce of me wanted to make sure she never looked at him that way again.

After she finally closed the door, I made my way out of the shadows and grabbed him. I pushed him into the darkness and he tried to fight me off, but he was no match for me. I had Romeo tie his hands and feet, and I tied a piece of cloth around his mouth to keep him quiet. We got him in the van that we had stolen and drove him out into the middle of the desert.

I had plans for him, and I didn't give a fuck what happened as long as I got to take him away from her.

Once we got to a place that we knew I wouldn't get interrupted, I opened the back of the van and pulled the fucker out. Scanning over him, I don't know what she fucking saw in him. If she didn't want to be part of the bad boy lifestyle anymore, she should have gone for someone who was clean cut.

This fucker had tattoo's stemming from his neck down to the tips of his fingers. My girl seems to have a type. He had on a chain hanging down from his jeans and I wanted to laugh at the fucking wannabe. He wouldn't know a damn thing about being a fuckin' hardass if he tried. His shit was all for show. She deserved better than that. Hell, she deserved better than me, but I wasn't giving her up.

Romeo kicked him once in the gut and he startled awake. He tries to say something, but it's all mumbled from the cloth in his mouth. I don't want to hear his shit so I don't bother taking it off of him. Pulling my knife out, I wipe both ends on my jeans before making my way towards him with it.

He tries to move, but it's no use. We never untied him.

"You put your hands on my girl, and I don't take lightly to that." He starts to struggle harder, but I don't care. He pisses himself and I hear Romeo chuckle. I grab him by the throat and run the blade of my knife down his chest before plunging it into his stomach. His eyes widen and he starts to scream even more loudly than before. Pulling my knife down, I watch as the blood starts to pour from him. He gurgles up blood and

I slide the knife back up into his chest cavity. I watch as the life bleeds out of him and I don't even feel an ounce of guilt. Knowing that his hands will never touch her skin again makes me feel a little bit better inside.

Pulling the knife from his chest, I wipe the blood off on my jeans and grab his phone. I go to his messages and find the one with her name on it. I see the last message he sent her and now I'm glad I fucking gutted the bastard.

I can't wait to get you alone tonight. I have plans for your sexy ass.

Pushing back down the anger that is threatening to spill out of me, I type out a message on her phone and pretty much ruin any chance he would have had with her.

Hey baby, I just got off work. I'm on my way home now.

I look down at the screen and wait for her to write him back, but she never does. She doesn't like cheaters, and I know that is exactly what she will think he is when she reads that message. Wiping my bloody glove on my pants, I toss the phone on him and Romeo cuts his ties and ungags him before we head out towards the van.

chapter Thirteen

"Stavros!" Romeo calls out. I shake my head and come back from the memory. Looking at him, I can see the concern on his face. "You good man?" I rub my hands over my face and sigh.

"I don't fuckin' know. My mind keeps running through memories of me and Harlyn and shit." My phone beeps, and when I look down at it, I see Harlyn's name across the screen.

Harlyn: **I need to talk to you.**

Instead of writing her back, I focus my attention back on my VP. "Did anyone find out any information?"

"No. Everyone that typically talks hasn't said shit. I think they finally caught on. They know better than to open their fuckin' mouths. Plus after word of Delilah got out there, some are afraid of that happening to them."

He doesn't say it like it's my fault, but I know that he's thinking that it is.

Yeah I probably shouldn't have sent them her body, but I was fuckin' pissed that they would even think about doing that shit to her.

"Get the boys out on the streets. I want to find out something, anything. Call in some markers if we need to. I want to know what they are planning before they attack." He nods and gets up from his chair. One thing I love about Romeo is that he never questions my orders. He does them, and makes sure to get the information I need before I put our plans in motion. He always has my back, even if I make stupid decisions, like killing that bastard in Vegas.

After he shuts the door, I contemplate being honest with Harlyn and telling her what I did. I know that it might make her run again, but if she finds out on her own, I have a feeling that it will be worse. Sighing, I get out of my chair and make my way out of my office and towards my room.

When I walk in, I see Harlyn laying against the pillows. She doesn't say a word as she watches me walk inside. Shutting the door behind me, I stalk towards the bed and lay down next to her.

"What did you want to talk to me about?" I look up at her from where I am, and she frowns.

"What would have happened if I didn't leave?"

Before I can answer her, she starts to speak again. "Would we still be happy together? Would I have been able to heal from the things I saw you do, or would I still be this broken version of myself that I left with?" She turns to face me and I can see the uncertainty written all over her face. I didn't know she was broken. She still walks and talks like the woman I let walk away. She is still the feisty woman that makes all this shit worth the darkness.

"I don't know." I reach out and cup her cheek, but it's not the answer she's looking for from me. I wish I could say that she wouldn't be broken after what happened if she stayed here, but I have no fuckin' clue. "I don't know what would have happened. What I do know is that I would have done everything possible to make sure that you were taken care of, and that you were happy the whole time. Were you happy while you were gone?"

A tear slides down her cheek, and she leans into my touch. "No. I was miserable. I wanted you to be there to hold me while I cried and had nightmares about that night, but you weren't. Instead I had to suffer through it all alone."

Pulling her into my lap, I wrap my arms around her and hug her tightly. "I would have been there if you needed me. I was always a call away. I hoped you would have called, but you never did." Blowing out a breath, I get myself ready to tell her what happened with that fucker that I killed for touching her.

"You remember the tatted up guy you were dating?" Her eyes meet mine, and she nods her head.

"What did you do?" She whispers.

"The first night you guys did, whatever, Cash called and told me that you were going home with that tool. I made the trip to Vegas with Romeo and when you two hung out the following night, I grabbed him outside of your apartment." Her eyes widen and she pushes away from me.

"You're the one who sent me that message from his phone." She starts to shake her head. She gets off the bed and starts to pace the room. "You did it because of me." She whispers when she looks up at me. "I was the one making you think that I was sleeping with him. It's all my fault."

Looking down at my hands as if they were covered in blood still, I can't help but feel sick. I need to just let her go. All I do is hurt her. Once this shit is dealt with, I'll let her leave. I won't force her to stay. "Harlyn, knowing that he was touching you ate away at me, and it was the only way I could deal with it. I'm sorry that I did it because he put his hands on you, but it would have happened either way because I don't let others touch what's mine." The tears start to fall down her cheeks, and I have to look away.

"You killed him because you couldn't handle knowing someone else was touching me? I can't believe you would do that." Her voice breaks and it stings all the way down to my toes. I really fucked up things with her and I know that there is no coming back from that.

"If you want to leave again after the lockdown is lifted and I know you're safe, you can. I won't stop you or try and get you back this time. I'll let you live the life you want. Cash won't follow you to report back, he will only be your protection." She nods her head and gets up and makes her way out of the room. She doesn't say another word, but I already know where she is going. Trix has always been her confidant while I've known her, and I don't expect it to be any different now.

One Week Later

Watching Harlyn from across the room, I can't help but want to go to her. She hasn't spoken to me since she walked out after I told her about killing that fucker. Trix found me the next morning and told me that Harlyn was really hurt and needed some space, so I granted it to her. She knows not to leave the clubhouse, so I'm not worried about her going anywhere without permission.

She bends over the bar and tries to grab something from behind it, and the only thing I can think of is the night I had her wrists bound above her head as I fucked her from behind on that very spot. I know she isn't bending over that spot on purpose, but I still can't help but imagine her there with her hands tied with her panties.

When she looks over her shoulder at me, I feel like I get the breath knocked out of me. She's fuckin' beautiful, and I wish I had the chance to run my hands over her body again. Her eyes linger on me longer than I expected them to. She doesn't move from her place, but she does grab whatever it is she was trying to reach and sits back on the bar stool. She grabs a glass off the bar and pours some of the liquor into her cup before shooting it back quickly and pouring more.

Instead of watching her get fuckin' hammered, I get up and make my way towards my office. On my way by Trix, I stop her and tell her to watch over Harlyn. When she drinks, she gets horny and wants to fuck like a wild woman. She walks away and nods her head. She knows her friend just like I do.

Closing myself inside of my office, I am able to get her out of my mind for a few minutes. Grabbing the bottle from my desk drawer, I pour myself a hefty amount from my new bottle of Johnny, and set the cup on my desk.

A text comes in telling me that they found out

some new information about when the Fighting Rebels are going to attack. Trent gives me the details, and I make a mental note to call all the men back in and hold church. We need to plan for this shit before it happens.

Sending out a text to Romeo, I tell him to get everyone back in tomorrow morning for church. His response is quick and also has more information than I expected.

Romeo: **I'll make sure everyone is there. Your ol' lady is getting hammered. She's hitting on everyone.**

Me: **I told her she could do what she wants after the lockdown is over.**

Romeo: **I'll believe it when I see it.**

His response doesn't surprise me because he knows me better than that, but this time I'm going to follow through with it for her.

Instead of focusing all my attention on her or my VP, I turn on the laptop on my desk and start to run some searches on Flint and his club. I don't find a whole lot, but I do manage to find out some information on the fucker that I can use against him if needed.

Before I can grab my phone to dial a number, my door bursts open and I see a very drunk Harlyn standing there. Watching her from my chair, I let her do everything. I know she's still pissed at me and if I make the first move, she'll just use it against me later.

She moves away from the doorway and pulls the door closed. "Stav." She whispers. Her body keeps moving towards me, and I can see the lust in her eyes. Her heel catches on the carpet and she starts to fall, but she rights herself before she can hit the ground. My hand reaches out to steady her, and she takes that time to pull herself towards me.

She straddles my lap and rubs her pussy against my dick. Closing my eyes, I try to fight my feelings for her, but I can't. Feeling her body pressed against mine brings out a need in me that I can't control. I want to grab her, push her up against the wall and fuck her hard like I used to, but I don't.

"I love you." Her whisper is like a fuckin' punch to the gut. It fuckin' kills me when she says things like that and doesn't mean them. In the morning there will be an awkward exchange, and an even harder goodbye as she leaves my bed to go back to Trix's room.

"Don't say it unless you mean it." I finally force out. Her eyes scan my face and she reaches forward to run her fingers down my cheek.

"I do mean it. I'm not that drunk Stav. I love you. I have since the first time I met you in this place, and no matter what stupid things you do, or the hurt that you cause me, it won't ever change." She leans forward and presses her lips to mine and I can taste the Jack Honey on her mouth.

My hands move up her back and she presses our bodies closer together. Looking into her eyes, I can tell she's drunker than she is stating, but part of me doesn't care as long as I get to be buried deep inside of her pussy.

"Please, Stav." At her words, my resolve breaks, and I pick her up.

"Hard or soft babe?" I ask, as I make our way towards my room. Kicking the door open, I wait for her answer, and when she finally gives it to me I toss her ass on the bed and kick the door shut behind me.

Crawling up the bed towards her body, I grip the edge of her shirt and pull it up, and over her head. Undoing her bra next, I slide it down her arms and toss it. When I move to her shorts, I pull them, and her panties, down before leaning forward to place a kiss on her stomach. Reaching above her head, I grab one of the bed cuffs and strap it to her right wrist before doing the same thing to her left. Kissing my way down her body, I put both of her ankles in the two at the bottom, and get off the bed.

She tries to fight against the restraints, but I like her best when she can't move. I like being in control of her body and being the one to make her come. She has no control this way and it gets me hard instantly. Her eyes watch me as I start to strip out of my own clothes, tossing them beside me on the floor. Before I make my way back to the bed, I walk over to my dresser, pull a few toys out, and make my way back towards her.

The crop I have in my hand is one of her favorite toys. I love watching her eyes light up just as I'm about to bring it down on her perfect skin. Setting the other toys down next to her left thigh, I sit on the other side of her, and run the crop over her thigh before I give her a slight slap. She moans and arches her back at the contact. I move the crop over her skin again for a second before I give her another smack. "Stav." She groans.

I smack her again, and this time she doesn't say a word. She just takes it and waits patiently for the next smack - but I don't give it to her. Instead, I run my fingers over her sweet, wet cunt, and slide my fingers through her juices. She's fuckin' dripping from just a couple of smacks. Before she left, I could smack her a few times before she got this wet.

Just as I'm about to latch onto her clit with my mouth, the door to my room swings open.

Chapter Fourteen

"Shit! Sorry." Dex says. Harlyn's breathing deepens and I slide my finger inside her pussy instead of my tongue.

"What?" I growl. I have fucking plans for my girl and he's interrupting them right now.

"Sorry Prez I –" I cut him off before he can start saying too much.

"Just fuckin' spit it out so I can get back to her pussy." I demand. I continue to thrust my finger into her and I can feel her getting wetter by the second. My body is blocking most of his view of her, but judging by the look on his face, he's having a hard time concentrating on what it is he's supposed to be telling me.

"We got some information about Flint and when

he's going to attack. Their plan is almost ready for execution and they are going to come storming in, guns blazing." I look at him and see him watching my fingers go in and out of her at a fevered pace. She's going to come any second, and I know he wants to watch.

"Have everyone meet in church in an hour." I groan out. Her whimpers fill the room and she cries out her release. "Get the fuck out." I bite out. He leaves without another word and turn my attention back to Harlyn. She has her face against her arm and she's breathing hard.

"You like him watching you as you come?" I nip at her skin as I make my way up her body. Her eyes meet mine, and I watch her for any indication that she is embarrassed or anything. Instead, her cheeks heat and she bites her bottom lip.

"Yes." Her voice is low.

"I want your mouth wrapped around my dick." I state. She nods her head eagerly, so I make my way up the bed so that my dick is right in front of her face. Grabbing the back of her head, I help her ease me into her mouth. I let her start the pace, but I slowly gain control. I force her to take me to the back of her throat and fuck her mouth.

She moans around my dick, and I love the vibrations that come from the back of her throat. Thrusting into her mouth quicker, I watch as she tries to catch her breath before I shove my cock down her throat again. When she starts to gag, I pull back and let her get the air she needs. She looks up at me and I feed her my dick again.

This time I fuck her mouth, not caring if she chokes or not. I feel my orgasm on the brink, and I can only think about one thing. When I spill my cum in her mouth, I watch her swallow it down as I pull out of her mouth. She tries to move her hand to my body, but in her position she can't reach me. Moving down her body, I capture her lips in mine, and I kiss her like I mean it.

I don't give her any warning as I push the head of my dick inside of her. Her eyes widen and she moans against my mouth. Her cunt squeezes the fuck out of me, but I can't help but love the feeling.

When I'm fully seated in her, I reach behind me and grab the vibrator. Turning it on, I run it over her body before sliding my hips to thrust in and out of her at the same time. If I had her tied up the other way, I would be fucking her ass while I fucked her with the vibrator, too. On second thought, that sounds even fucking better than what I'm doing now.

Pulling out of her, I hear her protest, but I slap her thigh, and she quiets down. I move to undo her feet and then her wrists before flipping her over and putting her limbs back in position. Sliding down her body, I make sure she's secured before I push her into the position I want her in.

Grabbing the vibrator, I run it over her pussy, and she starts to push back into me. Running my hand over her ass, I pull back and give her a slap. Her body moves forward and then she gets back where she was. I push the vibrator between her folds, her back arches up, and she moans out my name.

"Please, Stav." She begs.

Giving her what she wants, I pull the vibrator away from her pussy and slowly sink inside of her. Gathering up some of her wetness, I start to work my fingers inside of her ass before I slowly scissor my fingers inside of her. I work her hole a few minutes before I insert the vibrator into her, stretching her wide enough to take my dick.

Once I know she's ready, I pull out of her pussy and pull the vibrator out of her ass. Setting it on the bed for a second, I put the tip of my dick at her entrance, and start to push my way into her ass. I hear her hands moving and when I look up, she's gripping the blankets tightly in her fists. Once I get all the way inside of her tight little ass, I grab the vibrator and start to work her pussy over with it.

She cries out in pleasure and I start to fuck her ass hard. Leaning my body over hers, I place kisses on her back. Her grunts and moans fill the air and I can't help but pick up my pace. Just hearing the sounds coming from her get me hornier than ever. Biting down on her shoulder, she screams out my name as she comes. I thrust the vibrator in and out of her pussy as she rides out her orgasm, and fuck if it doesn't get me right on the edge.

She tenses and I can't hold on any longer. Pulling the vibrator out of her, I toss it on the bed and grip her hips. Each thrust is made of up long, hard strokes. "Stav." She moans.

Wrapping my fingers around her neck, I whisper in her ear, "I fuckin' love you." I give her throat a hard squeeze as I come inside of her. Her arms give out, and we both fall into the mattress. My body pushes into her and I can feel her heavy breathing. Reaching up, I undo the cuffs on her wrists and pull myself up to get the ones on her ankles.

She rubs her wrists as I lay on my back and stare up the ceiling. When she leaves, I'm going to be a fucking mess. Neither of us says a word, and I'm almost glad for the silence. Sure, it doesn't help the fuckin' voices in my head that tell me not to let her leave after all this shit is done, but I won't go against my word. I love her too much to trap her in this life against her will. Fuck - I'm starting to sound like a pussy.

She curls into my side and presses her cheek against my chest. Her leg is thrown over my waist, and my dick twitches. Her warm breath fans over my skin and I run my fingertips down her face. "Do you have to leave right now?" I lean my head down and kiss the top of hers before I answer her.

"Naw. I have a little bit of time. Why?"

"No reason really." I wrap my arm around her and close my eyes. I'm so fuckin' screwed.

My phone vibrates twenty minutes later and I can't bring myself to get out of bed to grab it. I watch the light on the screen dim for a minute before it starts to buzz again.

Finally pulling myself from Harlyn's grip, I grab my phone off the floor and hit the answer button. "Yeah?" I whisper. I don't want to wake her up.

"Thought we had church?" Romeo sounds pissed, but there isn't much I can do about that now.

"Be there in a second." I answer before ending the call. The fucker needs to get laid.

Getting dressed, I kiss Harlyn on the forehead before I make my way out the door and towards church.

When I walk through the doors, I see all my men looking antsy. I know this is the last place they want to be tonight, but now that we know they are going to attack, I want everyone ready for it.

"Thanks for coming. Dex brought some intel to me earlier." When I look over at him, I can see the smirk on his face. As much as I want to deck the bastard for seeing her in that position, I can't help but get hard just thinking about what I did to her earlier.

"Word is that they are coming at us while we're all here. I would like to get all the women and children into the underground storage area. The entrance is pretty well hidden from those who aren't privy to the location. The only thing I'm worried about is the ol' ladies being in the same room with the whores that are sleeping with their men." I watch E put his head in his hands, and Red looks down at the table.

"I don't give a fuck what you do, or where you stick your dicks, but everyone needs to keep the drama out of this fucking place until we get this shit handled and the families can go back home." The guys around the table nod their heads, and I move on from that topic.

I turn the table over to Dex so he can tell the guys what he needs done.

"I want to have a couple of men switching off on the lookout a few miles from the clubhouse. I want to know the minute they are on their way towards us. It will give us an advantage. I also want a few men standing guard at the gates. Everyone else will take turns switching out and such. I want everyone on guard at all times. I got in a new shipment of AR15's, and a few other guns that will do some damage." He grins while looking at all the men at the table before taking his seat again.

Dex has a thing for guns while I have a thing for knives. He's a crazy motherfucker if you try to cross him though, so I'm glad he's on our side.

"So, Dex and Romeo will work with everyone to make sure everyone has a detail and when they want you guys to switch. It's going to be a long few nights, but I don't want to risk anyone in our family. Posts must be manned starting tomorrow." I slam the gavel on the table, and everyone gets up from their chairs and start to make their way out of the doors.

Before I have a chance to stand up, E stops in front of Romeo and I. "Tina is a fucking loose cannon right now. I won't risk her being in the same room as Trix and Blade. If she fuckin' touches a hair on either of their heads I'll fuckin' kill her." I watch him carefully. I've never seen E this fucking wound up. He's typically the calm, cool, and collected one out of us all.

"You knew what you were doing when you fucked around with Trix." I state.

"Yeah I fuckin' know. I never meant it to mean anything, but it does. You and I both know that Tina is not the bitch for me. I only married her because she was pregnant and then a few months later she lost the baby, and leaving her wasn't a good idea. Ever since I found out about having a son a week ago, I can't think of anything else but them."

"He's eight months old." Romeo states.

"You've known about him since Trix turned up pregnant. Just because you wanted to believe that he wasn't yours all that time doesn't mean shit to us. You haven't done shit for that kid, and trust me, that will change. He's our family and if you don't take care of him, someone else will." E doesn't say anything at first, but I can see the look in his eye. He wants to challenge me.

"How the fuck would I have known that she was really carrying my kid? I wasn't the only one fucking her. She's a club whore." He shakes his head and I hope to fuckin' god he isn't as stupid as he's acting right now.

"She stopped fucking the brothers long before she became pregnant. Hell, she stayed the fuck away from here after I got her the other job. She only came around when you called her up. She's only had eyes for you for longer than I can remember, E. You want to keep stringing her along, then I suggest you move the fuck on. I won't let you hurt her or Blade any more than you already have."

He doesn't say anything, but he does look at Romeo, who has the same expression on his face that I'm sure I have right now. I made Romeo aware of everything I was doing for Trixie, and he agreed with me on it. He liked her and wanted to see her do better. Plus, I think he might have a thing for her. He's never said anything, but I see the way he watches her when no one else is looking.

"I won't let anyone else touch her." E barks out. Before I can stop Romeo, he pushes E against the wall, his forearm pressed tightly against his neck. I watch how it plays out because, honestly, I want to know how Romeo feels about her.

"You won't have a fuckin' choice." Romeo growls. "You have an ol' lady at home, and Trix sure as hell doesn't deserve to be just a play thing to you. Let someone who actually gives a fuck about her have a chance to make her happy. All you fuckin' do is make her cry."

E pushes Romeo back and I can see something new in E's eyes. He's fucking pissed, but he also has that look that comes when someone threatens you. "You fuckin' go near her, VP or not, I will end you. I won't let you take her, or my son from me." The both are staring each other down, neither of them giving up or showing any sign of walking away from this fight.

"Enough." I demand. Neither of them looks at me and when I put my hands on their shoulders and squeeze, I finally get their attention. "Neither of you get a choice. Trix is the only one who gets to make the decision. I will not let you two fucking try and destroy each other. I need everyone working as a fucking team. We have more important shit to deal with right now."

Turning on my heel, I make my way out the door, and leave them to it.

Chapter Fifteen

When I make my way back to my room, I open the door and I'm surprised to see Harlyn still laying in my bed. Instead of trying to figure out what she's going to do next, I just strip out of my clothes and let myself lay next to her. She may be gone in the morning, but I won't let that destroy me. My men need me.

Pulling her naked body into mine, I breathe in her scent. She turns in my arms and places her mouth to my skin. Her lips linger over the place on my heart and I close my eyes, relishing in the feel of it.

"Stav." Her quiet whisper brings my body to attention, and when I look down at her, I can see the hesitation in her eyes.

"Yeah?"

"Why do we continue to hurt each other?" Chills

run up my spine and I don't have an answer for her. "The whole two weeks I've been here, we've done nothing but fight, make up, fight, and fuck. That isn't me. I don't want to be that person. All I want is to go back to being the naïve girl you spent hours with. You told me things that I know for a fact you've never told anyone else. I bared my soul to you." Her voice trails off and I run my fingers over her cheek bone. The look on her face kills me.

"I want that too. I wish I could start over with you. I would have never subjected you to my lifestyle, and I sure as hell wouldn't have let anything happen to you." She stares at me, but doesn't move or say a word. I have no clue what is running through her head right now, and that's scares the fuck out of me.

"I love you Stav, but I can't be with someone who does what you do." My whole world feels like it's slipping through my fingers. I want to punch the fuckin' wall in anger, and I want to slit my own damn throat for hurting her so badly.

Closing my eyes, I release her, and roll over to my back. I don't have anything else to say. I know she won't give me the time of day anyway. She's made up her mind, and I'll do my best to respect that.

Instead of sticking around, I get out of bed and pull my jeans back on. Making my way towards the door, I take one last look at her before pulling it open and walking through it. I've always known that she deserved better than me, but I could never give her up. She was an addiction and my savior, all in one nice little package.

Coming to my office, I open the door and slam it shut. Sinking into my chair, I think back to one of my favorite memories.

The wind is blowing through her dark hair as she walks towards me. It's been a year since I claimed her, and I don't regret it for one damn minute. She has on a tight pair of jeans and a tank that has the words Draconic Crimson in bright pink letters. She had them made for all the ol' ladies and the whores. She wanted every woman that is part of this club to sport our logo, and I loved that.

She loves this club just as much as I do. Watching her walk towards me in those fuck me shoes she always has on give me a stiffy. I want to bend her ass over a damn chair and show her what she does to me, but I hold back. I always want everything between us to be fuckin' amazing.

"Stav." She purrs, running her finger down my

chest.

"Give me a kiss." I demand. She leans forward, licking her lips before she places her mouth on mine. Her tongue slips into my mouth and massages mine. Our kiss gets me hard as a rock and I pull her body towards mine. Her heels put her at just the right height for me.

"Take me shopping." She bats her eyelashes at me and I can't help but groan. I hate to shop. There is nothing worth spending fuckin' hours upon hours at a store just to find nothing. I only shop at one place and they have all the shit I need.

"You know how I feel about that shit." She gives me a pouty look and I almost give in.

"You promised." She says this time. Wracking my brain, I try to think of when I would have promised her that. "The other night when I gave you that blow job in front of everyone. I told you I would only if you took me shopping." She pulls away and crosses her arms. She gives me a look that's a cross between frustration and lust.

"Fine." I groan. "But first, I need you to take care of him." I point down to my dick and her eyes scan over the bulge in my jeans. He's begging for her touch and I know that she won't say no to me. She wants it just as much as I do.

She closes the distance between us and wraps

her arms around my neck, pulling our bodies together. I carry her to the first dark corner I can find. Lowering her to her feet, I press her into the wall. I pull her jeans down her legs and slide her panties to the side before pulling my dick out. Sliding into her sweet cunt, I fuck her hard against the wall until we both come.

By the time I pull the bike into the mall parking lot, I'm already regretting that fucking promise. The blow job was fucking amazing, but I would rather put a dull knife in my eye than shop with her. Cutting my engine, I help her off the bike and then secure her helmet. "Don't look so pissed." She giggles. She starts to walk off, but I grab her around the waist and pull her body back into mine.

"I am pissed. I hate shopping." I nip at her earlobe and she just giggles.

Wrapping my arm around her shoulder, I lead her towards that crowded fucking place that kids, teens, and adults alike go fucking crazy on shit that they probably don't even need, or that is priced way too damn high. She leads me through at least a dozen stores before she finds anything that she's even interested in.

The last store she drags me into is the lingerie store. Everything around us is lacey and see-through. Walking by a pair of panties that leave nothing to the imagination, I hold them up for her and she shakes her head at me. "Can you wear something like this?" I raise an eyebrow at her and she comes back over to me and wraps her arms around my waist.

"I'll wear whatever you want to buy me." I lean forward and press my lips to hers.

"My favorite words." I pick out a few sexy little outfits for her, and when she's done shopping for some of the things she wants for herself, we make our way towards the cash register. The woman behind it gives Harlyn a dirty look before running her eyes over me.

"You find everything you were looking for?" She drawls sweetly, pushing her chest out for me to see. I wrap my arm around Harlyn's neck and pull her into me before she has a chance to say something.

"Yeah. I can't wait to get her home so she can model it for me before it ends on my bedroom floor. If you know what I mean." I wink at the girl, and she starts to blush. Harlyn pinches me and I take her mouth in a bruising kiss.

After I pay for everything, I grab the bag and wrap my arm around Harlyn, leading her out of the shop and towards the exit.

"Thank you for everything Stav." She beams up at me.

"Anything for you baby." I kiss her lips before I shove her shopping bags into my saddle bags and close them. Handing her the helmet, I watch her put it on before I straddle my bike, and wait for her to get on behind me. Her legs squeeze around my hips, and her arms wrap tightly around my waist.

Looking up at the clock on my wall, I watch the hands tick. For what seems like hours, I just watch the clock move. The silence in my head is suffocating and as much as I want to do something about it, I don't. I don't deserve to keep fucking her up the way that I am. She's right; all we do is destroy each other.

For once, I want to be the man she needs.

Running my hands down my face, I blow out a breath and sit back in my chair. A soft knock sounds on my door and I yell for them to open it. When I see Trix walk in, I know that I'm going to hear something I probably don't want to know.

"Hey Stavros." She sets a sleeping Blade on the couch in the corner of the room before looking back over at me.

"What can I do for you babe?" I ask looking over at Blade. He looks peaceful, and I'm sure it's only a matter of time until shit gets messy between her and E.

"I want to leave Stavros. I can't stand watching her be all over him while I'm in the same room. I think I might deck the stupid bitch." She sighs and runs her hand over Blade's dark curls. "I don't get why he keeps her around when he hates her." This time when she looks up at me, I see the tears start to fill her eyes.

"You and I both know that he won't leave her. Babe, you need to do what's best for you and Blade. Stop waiting around for his ass. He isn't going to give you what you want." She frowns, but nods her head at my words.

"I just wish I was enough for him."

"Yeah I get you on that. I wish I didn't always fuck things up with Harlyn, but sometimes we just can't make it work no matter how hard we try." I sound like a fuckin' sap. Closing my eyes, I try not to focus on Harlyn. I need to start realizing that it's going to be over, or who fuckin' knows what will happen.

"She loves you Stavros. I don't think you two will ever be over." She gives me a small smile before looking back down at Blade.

"I have a feeling my VP has a thing for you." Her eyes meet mine and her eyebrows furrow together in confusion. She goes to say something, but can't get any words out.

"Romeo? No way. He can't possibly want someone like me." She shakes her head and I just grin at her. She doesn't know that Romeo went toe to toe with E, and as much as I want to tell her to move past E and his bullshit, I don't want to get involved. I'll always stand behind Trix, and the decisions she makes, but I won't be the one to help her to get to them.

"Romeo isn't the man you think he is. He's loyal, and a good fuckin' guy. But then again, E is Blade's father. Nothing will change that." She nods and I can see her thinking about things.

"What about you? You ever think about being a father?" Her question is innocent, but it hits me like a tons of bricks.

"Before shit went south, I thought about it. But now? Fuck - I don't know. I can't imagine it without Harlyn and as soon as the lockdown is lifted she's leaving so…" Fuck it. I won't even entertain the thought of being a father. I won't ever be one.

"What if things change?"

"She isn't going to change her mind, Trix. I'm already trying to come to terms with it. I rather not think about it." I open the drawer and grab the bottle of Johnny out of it, unscrew the cap, and take a big gulp. When I look back at Trix, she's shaking her head at me.

"Drinking isn't going to solve anything. If you want her, fight for her. She wants to know that you are going to be there for her when everything around you guys comes crashing down. She's afraid that being in love with you is going to be her downfall. What happens if you go to prison? What happens to Harlyn?" She gives me a stern look, and I get what she's saying.

Harlyn needs stability. She needs some fucker that can provide for her and her family one day. I want to be that man. Hell, I know I can provide for her, but I don't know if I can keep from ruining her more than I already have.

"What about you?" I ask. "You really want E?"

"I love him. I always have loved him. He's Blade's father, and I think I'll always be in love with him." She sighs, and then looks towards the ground.

"You know I just want you happy, right?" I walk over to her and wrap my arm around her shoulder and pull her towards me.

"I know." She says looking up at me. "Sometimes I wish I fell in love with you, or hell, even Romeo."

Loud gun fire starts, and I see Trix freeze. Grabbing my gun from the desk, I make my way towards the door, but stop before I walk out. "Go to Harlyn and stay with her." She nods her head and grabs Blade, holding him to her chest, she slowly makes her way to me, and we walk out the door. I push her towards my room and she slips through the door, just as another round of gun fire starts.

Running out towards the bar, I see my men start to push through the doors and out into the parking lot. Grabbing an AK47, I make my way outside and see the men from the Fighting Rebels standing right outside our gates. Why the fuck didn't anyone say anything.

Getting behind one of the pillars, I start to fire on them and I see a few hit the ground. My men start firing back again, and moving closer towards them. Once we level them all out, I see Romeo come running towards me.

"Where are Harlyn and Trix?" I just stare at him.

"What do you mean where are they? I sent Trix to my room to be with—" I take off running towards my room and when I open the door, I don't see anyone inside. "Harlyn? Trix?" I call out. I don't hear them say anything, but I hear a faint cry. Running towards my bathroom, I make my way inside and see Blade sitting in the shower. Picking him up, I soothe him the best I can, and make my way back towards my other men.

"It's a fucking diversion." I grit out. E comes running towards me and he reaches out and tries to take Blade, but he won't go to him.

"Where are the girls?" E asks, putting his arms down when he gets that Blade doesn't know him well enough to go to him.

"No fucking clue." I run my hand down Blade's back and he puts his head on my shoulder. "Romeo, get eyes on the ground. I want to know why we didn't know they were attacking, and I want to know where my fuckin' ol' lady and Trix are now!"

"I want Blade to stay with me." E finally states still staring at his kid.

"Keep your ol' lady away from him." I grit out. I would rather to have him with me, but E is his father, not me.

"She won't touch him. Swear on my life." I nod and hand him over. At first he tries to pull away, but after a few minutes he puts his head on E's shoulder.

chapter Sixteen

Six Hours. Thirty minutes.

The ringing of my phone forces me to sit the fuck down for a second. Checking the number, I see Trent's name on the screen. "Yeah?" I bark out. The only thing I want to hear right now is that he fucking knows where Harlyn and Trix are.

"Hey man. Still haven't heard a word on the girls. I have a buddy of mine trying to get information from a friend of his on the inside." Clenching my fists, I slam my fist on the desk and close my eyes.

"Fuck." I growl. "Just fucking find them." I hang up before he can say anything else. My patience is about shot, and I'm ready to call in the big guns if it helps me find my ol' lady. Looking down at where I set my phone, I contemplate picking it up and dialing the number. It's been years since I spoke to either of them, and I'm not even sure if they will answer.

Grabbing my phone, I search through the contacts until I see his number. Hitting the call button, I wait for him to answer the call. "Yeah?" his voice is rough and I barely recognize it anymore.

"Nikolai." I rasp out.

"Stavros?" he finally says after a few minutes.

"Hey little brother." I try to keep from saying anything else yet. There is a lot of shit running through my head right now, but finding Harlyn is my number one priority.

"What's wrong?"

"Why do you assume that something is wrong?" I ask. I hear his chuckle over the line, and I'm sure that he knows I wouldn't call if something wasn't wrong.

"Because, Stavros, I haven't spoken to you in years. There has to be something wrong if you are calling. What do you need?" He doesn't seem angered by it which is surprising.

"Someone kidnapped my ol' lady and one of the other girls. My men have searched fuckin' high and low and can't find them. I need help. I'm beggin' you Niko." I hear his sigh over the line and I have a feeling that he will turn me down, but he surprises me.

"Stav, you know I don't like getting involved in shit like that." His voice is tight.

"Niko, I can't fuckin' lose her. I love her. Please. I'm beggin' you, Niko. I wouldn't be asking if I had another choice. I'll ask Uncle Viktor if I have to." He sighs and sounds like he's getting out of bed or something.

"Don't. I'll help you. Let me make a few calls, and I'll give you a call back." He hangs up and I pull the phone from my ear.

A knock at the door breaks my attention from my phone, and I watch as E comes walking in with Blade. "You hear anything yet?" He asks as he takes a seat across from me.

"No, nothing yet. I made a call into someone who can probably help. Just waiting on a call back." I look at Blade, and see the dried tears on his cheeks. "How is he holding up?" I ask.

E looks down at him, and then back at me. "He's fussy as hell. He wants his momma. Fuck, I do too." He closes his eyes for a second and then looks back at me. "How the fuck are you not tearing this place down right now? You've never been good with your temper in times like these. Why the sudden change?" I look at the picture that Harlyn taped to my monitor three years ago, and I see her smiling face looking back at me.

"I'm barely hanging on. I'll kill Flint for even

thinking about touching her. I can't wait to gut the bastard with my knife, but getting angry now won't do shit. I need my head straight for when we get a location." He nods slightly and then looks back at Blade. "You have any problems with your ol' lady yet?"

"Naw, I told her if she came near him, I'd kill her. She seems to be taking the threat literally this time. I'm not fuckin' around with her. She won't ever be anything to him."

"Then why don't you just fucking cut her loose?" I ask.

"She threatened to kill herself if I did. I don't fuckin' want that shit on my conscience or Trix's. Trix doesn't deserve that shit and trust me man, I want to do right by her. I fuckin' love her." I nod my head, but before I can say anything my phone starts to ring.

"Yeah?" I answer.

"Prez there is someone out here asking for you." One of the prospects says.

"Who?" I bark out. I don't have time for anyone's bullshit.

"He's driving some nice ass fuckin' beamer. He just said he needed to see you." Getting out of my chair, I make my way towards the door with E following behind me.

Shoving my phone in my pocket, I pull out my gun, and open the doors to the clubhouse. When I see the car, I see the man with his back to me. When he turns around, he smirks at me and then raises an eyebrow. "You know better than to pull a gun on your brother, Stavros." Putting my gun in the back of my jeans, I walk over to Nikolai and pull him into a hug.

"Thank you for coming." I say as he hugs me back. He isn't nearly as tall as I am, but he definitely got bigger over the years.

"I couldn't let my big brother destroy the whole fucking town trying to find his ol' lady." He slaps me on the back and when we pull away, I see my men staring at him.

"Boys, this is my brother Nikolai. Nikolai, these are my brothers." He nods to them all, but doesn't say anything.

"I need to talk to you, brother." He states. I nod my head and lead him to my office.

"What?" I ask. I know he has some kind of information for me.

"I think I might have found them. I have a friend of mine digging a little to verify the location." I go to walk past him towards the door, but he stops me. "No. Stav. I need you to keep your fucking head on. You can't go in fucking guns blazing. That's what they are waiting for. They want you dead. I don't know what you fucking did to the bastard who runs that fucking club, but he has it out for you."

Punching the wall, I turn toward Niko and he just watches me. "How the fuck do you expect me to just stand around here twiddling my fuckin' thumbs while that fucker and his rejects have her. Who the fuck knows what he's doing to her right now while we do nothing." I grit out.

"I get you're fucking pissed, but going in blind will only get you killed. I'm trying to protect you." He puts his hand on my shoulder and I shrug it off.

"Yeah fuckin' right. You are only here because I begged you. You wouldn't have fuckin' cared otherwise. You've been probably waiting for me to fuck up so you can come and clean up my mess." I walk over to my chair and sink down into it.

My eyes flit back over to the picture of Harlyn and my heart aches. Rubbing my hand over my chest, I look up to see my brother's curious eyes.

"I've never seen you this hung up on a girl, even in high school." Dropping my hand, I look over at the door before turning my attention back to him.

"She's it for me. After this, I know she isn't going to take me back, but I need to know that she will be safe. That no one will ever hurt her again." He takes a seat across from me and puts his elbows on his knees.

"What do you mean? She was taken from here, isn't she your ol' lady?"

"She was. She left a year and a half ago after I gutted a man in front of her. I had one of my men drag her ass back here for her protection when threats were made against her by Flint, the president of the Fighting Rebels. I thought I had her in my grasp again, but I fucked it all up already." I put my head in my hands and I rub my face.

"I don't get why you even bother with an ol' lady. You are the president of an MC. You can get any pussy you damn well please, and you're hooked on some bitch's pussy?" Before I can say anything back to him his phone rings.

"What do you got?" he grunts out a few answers that I can't make out. I check my phone and it's blank. Fuck, I just want to know that she's okay.

"No. Get my uncle on the phone." He growls. My eyes meet his and I try to get a read on him but I can't. His expression is stone and he looks pissed. "What the fuck is going on Viktor? I told you that I needed it done today and you sent my men somewhere else." He listens to what Viktor is saying and I can't be jealous that he's dealing with that bullshit and I'm not.

"Get them where they belong now. I have shit I'm dealing with. I'll deal with the rest when I get back." He bites out.

He pulls his phone away from his head and hits another button to do, who the fuck knows what. "Give me something." He demands. He listens for a second before he gets up, and motions for me to follow him. "Where is there a map?" I walk him towards church where we have a map of the town hanging behind my chair with all our territory outlined.

He makes his way over to it and puts his finger on a spot before he continues to talk to whoever the fuck is on the other line. Romeo comes up beside me and just watches for a second.

"Didn't know you had a brother." He states. We both watch what he's doing on the map and I don't even bother to reply. "You guys look almost like you could be twins."

"Yeah, I know. We heard it all the time growing up." I watch Nikolai circle a spot on the map a few times before he hangs up and walk over to us. "What do you have Niko?"

"Got word on where they have the girls. They have it fucking secured like Fort fuckin' Knox. We need a plan for attack. There is no fuckin' way we are just walking through the front door." He eyes Romeo, but he doesn't say anything else.

"I'll give myself up for them." I state. They both look at me and shake their heads.

"You have no fucking clue if he even wants you."

Romeo states. Instead of listening to him, I grab my phone and dial the number I got from Trent. It rings four times before I hear him pick up.

"Well, well. I see you figured out that you can't get into this place." I hear Harlyn scream out in the background. Closing my eyes, I force the monster in me to stop trying to break free. I need to stay level headed until I can get Harlyn to safety.

"I'll take their place." I say through gritted teeth.

"Now, now. I am really looking forward to having a party with your ol' lady, Stavros. Nice touch, inking her skin with your name. The other bitch belongs to one of your men right? That kid I left behind is one of theirs?"

"Leave her the fuck out of it. You want someone, come and get me. You leave them alone. They didn't do shit. They're innocent." Niko comes up behind me and puts his hand on my shoulder. His grip on my shoulder tightens the angrier I get, and it somehow calms me enough to keep dealing with this bastard.

"I'll let this other bitch go in exchange for you, but I rather keep this pretty little thing that you claimed as your own." The blood drains from my face and I know what he's going to do. He'll have me watch what he does to her. Clenching my hands, I tell him the only deal I'm making.

"You can have me for them. That's the only thing

I'll give you. I don't care if I live or die, but you won't hurt a hair on either of their heads."

"As much as I want you to die a slow painful death, I'm not sure I want just you. I rather make her watch as I bleed the life out of you. She will stay safe for as long as you stay alive." I look at Romeo and Niko and they both shake their heads at me.

Before I can let them change my mind, I answer him. "Deal." They both give me dirty looks, but I don't let them affect me. "One of my men is coming with me on the trade to get her back safely."

"Fine. One wrong move and I'll shoot her on the spot." He hangs up without another word.

chapter Seventeen

Pocketing my phone, I turn to face them and they both have masks of anger covering their faces. "I don't give a fuck what either of you says. I'll die for her." Niko walks over to the wall and punches it. Romeo looks between us, but doesn't say anything. He knows that my mind is made up, and there is no way he'll change it now.

"You a fucking idiot Stav. How the fuck does one girl mean this fucking much to you. You're fuckin' throwing the rest of your life away for some bitch." He shakes his head and walks out of church. I look over at Romeo and although I know he doesn't disagree with my brother's statement, he doesn't say anything either.

"I need you to find a way to save her. I owe it to her to make sure she stays alive, Romeo. Please." He looks at me for a hard minute before he nods and reaches his hand out towards me. Grabbing it, I pull him into a hug and whisper in his ear. "I owe you a shit load. I'll never be able to repay you. You've been my best friend and right hand for far longer than I deserved. Thank you." He pulls away and claps me on the back one last time before he walks out too.

Sinking into my chair, I look out at the table and try to not focus on what I just did. My phone beeps with a message and when I check it, it has a time and place. Tapping my hand on the table, I get up and make my way out towards the guys.

Everyone is already standing around since I'm sure they know about my plan. Sometimes these guys are worse than gossipy bitches. All eyes are on me when I walk up. Nikolai is standing at the bar with a glass of what looks like bourbon. His eyes meet mine and they don't look as pissed as before.

"I'm sure you've all heard that I'm trading places with Trix. Flint agreed that he won't kill Harlyn as long as he has me, and I stay alive. Do me a favor boys and save her." E comes up to me and pulls me into a hug that has his ol' lady storming off with a pissed off expression.

"Thank you." His voice breaks and I know for sure that he feels something about Trix. Now I just hope he doesn't let this second chance pass him by.

"Don't thank me. Just do right by her." He nods

when I pull away and I walk over to Nikolai.

"I know you don't agree brother, but I can't not do anything. I've made a lot of mistakes and enemies over the years - I have to save her. She was right. My sins are the ones that are going to destroy us. I just hope that she only walks away with scars. My death won't be in vain if she lives. Don't let her fend for herself." I don't wait for his reply.

I walk over to Romeo and put my hand around the back of his neck and pull him in so I can say one last thing to him. "I want you to take my place. The men respect you, and I know that you'll do right by them." He nods and I turn to walk towards the door.

"Dex." I call out. He appears to my left and I motion for him to follow me out towards the bikes. One last look around the room, I see the shock and anger written all over their faces. They have no fuckin' clue how much I owe to them. I wouldn't be half the man I am without these fuckers. They've carried me through so many shitty times.

"Hopefully I'll see you guys soon." I turn to look at Nikolai and Romeo once more before I walk out the door and follow Dex to our bikes.

"Make sure you get Trix back home to her little boy." He nods and starts his engine. Starting mine, I look back at everything I've built over the years.

We take off into the night and when we pull into

the lot at the address, I see a van start to make their way towards us. I hear Dex grab his gun and click the safety.

The van stops and I see them get out along with a bruised Trix. When her eyes meet mine, I try to be reassuring. Tears fill her eyes and I make my way towards them. "Let her go." I bark out. He pushes her towards me and I grab her, pulling her into my body. "Dex will take you back. How's my girl?" her lips trembles and she holds tightly to me. I walk over to Dex's bike and check her over.

"They busted open her lip. Other than that I think she's okay. Please get her back." She whimpers, as I hand her off to Dex and I motion for him to get the fuck out of here.

I watch them speed off before anyone can go after them, and then I turn to face Flint. "You got me. Now what?" I taunt. I know he isn't going to go easy on me, but part of me doesn't care. I'll answer for all my sins if I have to. I just hope like fuckin' hell they save Harlyn.

"You have no idea what I plan on doing to you." He grins. He starts to walk towards me and I tense up. He tries to punch me and I put my fist into his stomach. He hunches over, and two of his men take me to the ground. My chin hits the ground hard and I know I'll probably have a fat lip, but I don't even care.

"Maybe I'll even make you watch as I gut your girl." He grins and I fight to get free of his men. A knee to my back keeps me in place even though I try like fucking hell to get to him again. When I get free, I'll be sure to shove a knife in his throat.

"Get him in the van." I feel a prick in the side of my neck and everything starts to fade to black.

Waking up, I try to lift my head up, but I can't. My whole body feels heavy and I can barely keep my eyes open. My head sways side to side a bit and I finally see a little bit of movement to my left. "Harlyn." I rasp out.

A whimper comes from her and when I try to look in that direction, I can't. My head lolls back towards the ground and my eyes shut. "Stav." I can hear her sweet, scared voice, but the darkness is pulling me towards it again. I can't do anything but listen to her soft cries. "Stav, I'm so sorry. I shouldn't have pushed you away. Maybe then we wouldn't be here in this mess." Her soft cries turn into sobs and I want so fuckin' bad to go to her, but my body just won't fuckin' work.

Fighting like hell to open my eyes, I'm finally able

to turn my head enough to see her chained to a wall to my left. Her clothes are dirty and she has dried blood on her mouth. "Don't be sorry babe." I whisper hoarsely. "I don't regret a minute with you. Good or bad."

I try to move my hands, but I'm tied to something. "What am I tied to?" I ask her. She sniffles a few times before she gets out the words.

"A table of some sort. I don't really know." She whimpers. The door opens and I hear booted feet coming towards us before the door slams shut.

"Looks like your finally awake Stavros." A hand grabs me by the neck and forces my head upright. For the first time since being in here, I can see in front of me. Flint has a wide grin on his face as he looks over at Harlyn. "She sure is prettier than I remember. You know Stavros, I remember being jealous that a crazy mother fucker like you could pull this hot little number, but now? Not so much. If she likes crazy, I can show her even more than you ever did!"

He lets go of my neck and I can't keep my head up, so it falls back down. I try to watch him as he makes his way towards her. He grabs her face and runs his tongue down her skin. I try to jerk my body out of the restraints, but they don't fucking move. Clenching and unclenching my fist, I try everything I can think of but it's no use. "A deal is a fuckin' deal." I grit out. His laughter fills the room, and I hear her soft cries again.

"No one ever said I was good at keeping my word." I hear a crack of what sounds like him hitting her, and her crying out in pain. When I finally get my head to turn towards her again, I see the fresh blood falling down her face.

"I'll fuckin' kill you." I grit out. I thrash as much as I can against the restraints again, but I don't move.

"Looks like you won't be doing much of anything, Stavros. I can't wait to hear her screams fill up the room. And maybe I'll even let you see how much you took from me." He grins and pulls something out of his jeans before coming back over to me. "I know how much you like this knife." He shows me the blade to my knife before he runs the sharp edge across my skin. My skin burns as he slices me open. I grit my teeth, but don't give him what he wants.

He wants me to beg him for my life, but I won't. The longer I hold out, the safer she is.

When he doesn't get the reaction he wants from me, he wipes the blood on my jeans before making his way out of the room. The door slams shut behind him and I finally hiss out under my breath. "Fuck." The more lucid I become, the easier it is to get my head up and look around the room. The cement walls make it hard for anyone to get to us, and I can only imagine where this fucking place is.

"Harlyn." I groan.

"Stav." She whimpers. Closing my eyes for a second, I try to keep my voice even.

"I'll get us out of here." I vow. I'll do anything to save her.

"I don't want to lose you." She whispers. Turning my head towards her, I look over her body. This time she has a hole in the jeans she's wearing and I know he ran my knife over them.

"Harlyn, I know I was a shitty man for you, but just know that I will give my life to protect you. I love you baby and nothing will ever change that." I hear her choke out a sob and I hate that I'm the reason she's even in this mess.

"I love --" the door slams against the wall, and I watch as a few of Flint's men come walking into the room. One walks over to Harlyn, and I try to struggle again, but it's no use. I hear the fuckers snicker, but I don't give a fuck. I want to get that bastard away from her.

Before the door shuts again, I see Flint make his way inside. He comes right at me and puts his fist into my stomach. I let out an 'oomph' and try to suck in a breath. I feel blood start to pour from where he sliced my skin, but I don't let it affect me. I watch as they all start to gather around me.

"Turn the table. I want her to watch." They start to turn the table and I finally get a good luck at Harlyn.

She has a cut by her eye, and it's bruised. Flint better hope I don't get away from them. I will make him and every other fucker pay for even touching her.

He grabs the knife and walks over to her. I watch as he puts the blade to her throat and memories from the past flood my head. My vision starts to go hazy with thoughts of the last fucker who put a knife to her throat, and what I did to him.

She whimpers as he pushes it into her skin and I clench my fists.

One of the guys grabs a blow torch and walks over to Flint. He whispers something to him and I see Harlyn's eyes widen. She looks at me and fear takes over her features. One of the other's comes up with a metal bar and I already know what they plan on doing. Harlyn gives me a terrified expression and I have a feeling that she knows exactly what they are going to do to me.

Dumb fuck number one lights the torch, and Flint takes the bar from the other and grabs a glove, pulling it on. He takes the torch and gets the bar as hot as he can before putting it near Harlyn. Tears start to stream down her face and I yell out, "So help me fucking God, if you touch her with that I'll hunt you all down and gut you like fuckin' pigs." Flint grins, walks it over to me, and touches it to my ribs.

The searing pain of the hot metal has me gritting

my teeth and gasping to catch my breath. The pain is almost unbearable, but I would rather take it than let him hurt her. "Stav!" She cries out. When he pulls it off of my skin, I drop my head, and breathe harshly through gritted teeth. "Stav!" She cries out again.

When I look up at her, I can see all the emotions running through her pretty features. She has tears streaming down her face and she tries to hit the guy next to her, but he ends up backhanding her instead.

The blow torch starts again and I watch as the metal heats up to an angry red color. Once it's done, he presses the metal into my skin under my left pec. I grunt out in pain and I see my skin burn, and practically melt around the metal bar. The smell of burnt flesh fills my nose, and all I can hear is Harlyn's screams.

"Stop! Please stop!" she cries out. My eyes meet hers and I can see the pain in them before I pass out from the excruciating pain ripping through my body.

Chapter Eighteen

A slap to the face brings me to. Looking around the room groggily, I see a few of the men from earlier. When I look up, I see Harlyn curled into a ball on the ground. She isn't moving and I have no fucking clue if she's alive or not. The door opens and I hear someone walking towards me. When I see them finally walk around from behind me, I see a small table being set on the floor next to Harlyn and a tattoo gun being set on it.

My eyes follow the man and I watch as two men pull her off the ground and sit her in a chair on one side of the table. Her eyes meet mine and this time she isn't crying. "As cute of a thought it is that she has your name tattooed on her, I think it's quite shitty. If I decide on keeping her alive after I do away with you, I want to make sure that she knows that she doesn't belong to you anymore. I'm going to make sure she knows she belongs to me."

He grabs her wrist and sets it on the table and the guy starts the gun. "Don't fuckin' touch her." I growl. He looks between us before he whispers something in her ear. Her body turns ram rod straight and she looks over at me and pleads with me to stop fighting. "Harlyn, don't let him." I demand.

"I have to." She whispers brokenly. He grins at me and motions for the guy to start, but I thrash against the table again.

"No you don't! You can fight him baby." She quickly shakes her head no and I watch as she gives the guy her wrist. "Harlyn don't!"

"He'll kill you if I don't." A tear slides down her cheek, and she looks away from me as the buzzing starts. Closing my eyes, I can't watch. The metal bar that is across my chest leaves no room for me to move and my legs are shackled to the bottom. My wrists are shackled into place, too, or I'd fucking strangle the bastard if he got close enough.

By the time he's done with his little show of ownership over Harlyn, he walks back over to me. "She sure does look better with my name on her body." He puts his face in mine, and I hit him as hard as I can with my forehead. He stumbles back and then walks over to her and grabs her by the neck. He brings her closer to me, and I want so bad to reach out and touch her.

"Do you want to watch me fuck her?" she

whimpers and I just watch her. Her eyes land on the burn on my side and then moves to the one under my pec. Tears fill her eyes and she reaches out to touch my skin. Her cold hands are like a shock to my system and I want to break both of his hands for even touching her.

He pulls her away from me and I struggle against the restraints. He pulls my knife out and brings it to her neck again. My eyes follow his movements and someone hands her another knife. She shakily takes it from him and I watch as Flint whispers something else in her ear. Her eyes snap to mine and they widen. She looks terrified, and I just wait for him to say something.

"Go ahead bitch. Just remember what'll happen if you don't." Her naturally tan skin pales, and she looks at me with remorse.

"Baby, look at me." I whisper. Tears start to fill her eyes again and I nod at her. "Do it. It's okay." If her doing this saves her life, then I'm okay with it. She closes her eyes and presses the knife to my stomach. Her lips trembles and I want to take away all her pain, but I can't. There isn't a damn thing I can do for her right now. She pushes a little harder and I feel the blade start to sink into my skin.

Clenching my fists, I suck in a breath and wait for it to be over. When she pulls the knife back out, I feel the warm trickle of blood as it starts to cover my skin. Her eyes scan over my stomach and she cries out. "Again." He demands. She shakes her head no, but he grabs her hand and forces her to stab me again. Her body is hunched over mine from the force he used to push the knife into me. Her tears fall against my naked skin, and she wraps one of her arms around my neck.

"I'm so sorry." She sobs. I try to swallow, but my mouth is dry. All I can feel is the pain as it radiates through my body. Her lips press to my neck and she's pulled away before I can say anything to her.

Standing about ten feet from me grabbing Harlyn by the arm, I see Flint motion for his men to take their turns. I take blow after blow on my ribs, my face, and my chest. Every hit to the face feels like it breaks a bone, but I don't make any noises unless it's to breathe.

Harlyn begs them to stop, but nothing she says gets the blows to cease. They want to see how far they can beat me down before I give up. But what they don't know, is that I would do anything to make sure she lives through this. A boot to my chest knocks the breath right out of me, and I feel my body start to shut down. The monster in my chest is begging to come out to play, but I couldn't let him free if I tried. Staying alive is the only thing I can do right now.

She breaks free from Flint and starts hitting the guy that's about to kick me in the stomach again. He wraps his arms around her and pulls her into his body. "I'm not afraid to give you a little something." He thrusts his hips into her body and she gets pale. She kicks her leg and nails him in the dick, causing him to release her. She runs over to me and wraps both arms around my neck, and cries on my shoulder. Her face buried in my neck.

"Stav please don't give up. Save us. Please." She begs. I turn my head to kiss the side of her face, and see Flint watching us. He doesn't let his men come near us, for once. I know that they are going to do something to her for attacking that bastard, but I can't bring myself to worry about that when I have her body so close to mine. I know that it won't last long, but any moment I can get with her before they end my life is worth all the pain.

"I love you Har. Never forget that." She nods her head against my neck, but doesn't move. "Romeo and Nikolai will find you and save you." Her head pops up and she looks into my eyes.

"No." she shakes her head. "No, you're not leaving me. Not now. Not after all of this." Flint pulls her off of me and forces her out of the room with him. Her screams are heard throughout the concrete room, and I can't imagine what he's doing to her right now.

My bare feet are put into buckets of water and I watch as they bring over what looks like a cattle prod. Flint comes back in the room with Harlyn, and this time, she looks out of it. Her eyes are half way closed and I can only imagine what they gave her. He sits her on the ground by the wall and her eyes meet mine. They widen a fraction when she sees what they've done. Flint grabs the cattle prod and starts walking towards me.

As soon as it touches my skin, I feel the jolt of electricity run through me. Every muscle in my body contracts and I hold my breath until he pulls it off of me. I gasp out a breath and my heart is racing. I'm not sure how much more of this shit my body is going to be able to handle. I just fuckin' hope that Romeo and Nikolai find her before it's too late.

The cattle prod touches my skin again and I feel my whole body shake uncontrollably. My teeth chatter and I'm pretty fuckin' sure I just bit my tongue. My hands clench and I try to keep myself conscious, but I'm having a hard time. When it finally stops, my head falls forward, and all the muscles in my body go limp. My labored breathing is the only thing I can focus on.

"Bring her with us. Let's let our boy have some time to himself." I can't even fight the boneless feeling in my body right now. I wish I could stop them from taking her from me, but I can't.

I've never been the type of man to pray to a higher power, but right now I would do anything to make sure that Harlyn was protected. The door slams shut and I can't hear anything but my labored breathing. I don't know how long I just stare at nothing before I can even get a word out.

"Please God. I know I've been a shitty as fuck human being over the years, but please don't let that affect her outcome from this shitty situation. Please help Nikolai and Romeo find a way to get to her and save her before it's too late. She deserves all the fuckin' happiness that I couldn't provide for her over the years. I didn't deserve to ruin her the way I did." My head hits against the table as I look up at the wall. My eyes are having a hard time staying open.

Before I can close my eyes, I hear the door open again and then shut quickly. I hear her cry out in pain. "Harlyn." I whisper hoarsely.

I hear her bare feet slap against the concrete floor as she runs over to me. She runs her fingers over my face and she has a sad look on her face. "Stav." Her whimpers fill the silent room and I wish I could do something - anything.

Her hand moves down to one of the stab wounds in my stomach and she puts her hand over it. "You're losing a lot of blood." She whispers. Her eyes meet mine again and my head falls forward. She grabs my face and forces my head up. "You can't die, Stav. Please don't leave me. Who knows what they'll do to me if you die." I wish I could reach out and touch her face once more.

Every inch of my body is screaming out in pain, and part of me wants it to be over, but the other part wants me to fight for her. Fight for us even though I know that there won't be an us in the future.

"I… I … I'll try babe." I finally choke out. I start to cough and I can taste the blood as it starts to pool in my mouth. I cough again, and this time I end up getting it on her hands that are still holding my face up.

Her lip trembles and she puts her forehead against my collarbone. She silently sobs against my skin and I wish that there was something I could do for her right now. My eyes are getting heavy and I start to cough some more. I see blood spatter against her again, and I want to push her away from me, but she wouldn't let me even if I could.

"I'm sorry my sins have touched you. I never meant for this." I say in a ragged breath. I think one of the kicks to my stomach or my chest broke a rib. Breathing hurts, and I might have even passed out for a few seconds from the pain.

Someone comes in, who the fuck knows how long after, and releases me from the table. I fall to the ground and Harlyn pulls me into her body. Everything feels like jello since I haven't moved in, who fuckin' knows how long. I lay in her arms until I can start to get movement back in my limbs.

Wrapping an arm around her waist, I pull her to me, and hug her. Burying my face into her hair, I breathe in her scent once more. I don't know when I'll get another chance to memorize her, let alone hold her like this.

"You have to save us." She whispers again. I try to stand, but I can't force my body to work with me. After a few tries, she stands up and tries to pull me up with her. When I finally get on my feet, I sway a few times, and almost knock us both over. My hand goes to one of my stab wounds and I see the blood still trickling out of me. I've lost a lot of blood, and I'm not sure how much longer I'll be able to keep upright like this. Hell, I'm surprised I'm still conscious right now.

When the door opens, one of the Fighting Rebels walks in and shuts the door behind him. He comes towards Harlyn and I know it's the bastard that said he wasn't afraid to give her a little something of himself. When he grabs her, I release her and grab the knife out of the holder he has connected to his jeans. Using a lot of my fuckin' energy, I unsleeve the knife and thrust it up, and into his back. Covering his mouth with my hand, I feel his teeth sink into my skin as he tries to fight me. Pulling the knife back out, I shove it in right where his neck and spine connect, and he goes limp in my arms.

We both fall to the ground, and I try like fucking hell to get the knife out of him. Harlyn squeaks out and then comes over to me and helps me up again. "I need the knife babe. It's the only way I'll stand a chance against them." She looks back and forth between me, and the guy that has the knife stuck in his back. Harlyn grabs the knife and pulls it out. She hands it over to me and I walk with her away from his body. Her hands cover her face and she hides in my neck. My free hand runs down her back and I move us against the wall, sinking us onto the floor. I hold her in my arms until the door opens again a while later.

Chapter Nineteen

My hand absently runs over the tattoo that he forced her to get. When I look down at it, I see his name written on her skin, and the monster inside of me wants to gut the fucker for even trying to take her from me. When the door opens, I see Flint's eyes scan the room. He sees his man on the ground and I can't help but grin at him.

Harlyn moves out of my lap and sits on the ground next to me, watching as Flint comes further into the room. His eyes never leave me and that makes the monster inside of me ecstatic. Not that I can really move all that much. Every move takes way more effort than it should, but I won't let that stop me from gutting this bastard like the fuckin' pig he is.

As he moves closer to us, I slowly get to my feet. "I see you got some of your anger back. That's good."

He grins. He looks over at Harlyn and reaches his hand out to her. "Come, my dear." She shakes her head no and he reaches down to grab her. Pulling the knife out, I grab him by the neck and push him back into the wall behind him. My fingers flex around his neck and I want so bad to crush his wind pipe, but that would let him off too easy.

I want to make him suffer like he's been making me and Harlyn suffer.

The knife slices his skin quickly as I recreate what he did to me. The only difference is I push the knife into him deeper than he did to me. He yells out, and before I can get any further, men start storming in the room. Grabbing him around the neck, I walk backwards towards Harlyn, keeping the knife firmly against his neck.

"Let me go and I won't make her suffer too much." His voice is nothing more than a few gasps, but I don't release him. I don't give a fuck what he says; there is no way I'll let him go. When I do, I'll be right back against that table, unable to protect Harlyn from these fuckers.

"I'll gut you before I let you go." I feel my body start to wheeze and I know I won't be able to keep it up much longer. My body is giving up, and I feel like I'm failing her.

Just as I'm about to thrust my knife into his

throat, I feel something hit me, and the electrical jolt knocks me on my ass. Flint pulls himself off of me as my whole body starts to twitch. Every muscle in me is being fucking shocked to hell. Harlyn goes to touch me, and when her hand touches me, I see her eyes widen as it must have shocked her too. It stops, and my whole body goes limp on the cold, hard ground. My eyes close, and the last thing I hear is Harlyn screaming out my name as someone grabs her and drags her away from me.

A knife digs into my skin and my eyes fly open. Trying to move, I realize that I am now strapped back down to the table. Breathing heavily, I look around the room and try to find Harlyn. When I don't see her anywhere, I look at Flint running the knife across a big part of my chest.

The burning sensation as my skin splits open makes me grit my teeth, but I still don't give him the satisfaction of knowing that he's got me where he wants me. "Where is she?" I grit out.

"I have her in my room. I plan on finally taking her after the shit you pulled. You killed my sergeant at arms." I spit at him and he just pushes the knife deeper into my skin. My vision gets hazy and I pass out again.

I awake to another beating, but it doesn't even matter anymore. If he hurts her, everything I've done will be in vain, and there is nothing I'll be able to do to protect her anymore. Blow after blow brings me in and out of consciousness. Nothing I do can keep my body from shutting down. I can feel the blood sliding down my face and dripping onto my chest. Every hit brings me closer to the end, and I know that at least I went out with a fight.

I tried to save us both, but I couldn't. My eye swells and I can barely even see out of it anymore. My whole body aches and I know that they aren't even close to being done with me. They're still trying to figure out how much I can take before they kill me.

Flint brings a knife over with him and slices through my skin. Everything around me goes black, but I can hear Harlyn screaming for me. They brought her back into the room, just so she can watch them kill me. I want to be there to hold her and tell her that everything will be fine, just like I did the night I brought her back after that bastard kidnapped her.

Fuck, I'd give anything just to feel her body against mine one more time. She has no fucking clue about the color she brought into my grey and fucked up world. I'll never get to see her belly grow with my kid, and I sure as hell won't get to kiss my way down her body as she moans out my name.

Every good memory flashes through my head, and I'm able to hold on to one moment that stands out against the rest.

"Harlyn I hate pictures." I groan. She's straddling my lap, and the only thing she wants to do right now is take a picture of us with this new fucking Polaroid camera I bought her earlier. We were out at the mall after I, somehow, got conned into taking her shopping, again. She found the damn thing and begged me to get it for her. She knows I can't say no to her, but she sweetened the deal anyway.

"Please Stav. I want to be able to always remember this perfect day with you. Please." She pokes out her lower lip, and I lean forward to bite it. She grins and kisses me with all the passion in the world.

"Fine." I grunt out. We are still connected from the sex we just had a few minutes ago and she hands me the camera. I pull her down on me and she gives the camera a kissy face while I suck on her neck and hit the button. The flash is fucking bright and the camera spits out the picture. She pulls it from the top of the camera and lays her head on my chest as we wait for it to develop.

She's fucking beautiful. She's the fucking color in the dreary life I've lived for the last ten years. Never have I wanted something as much as I want her. She squeals when she sees the photo and kisses me deeply. "I love it. It's perfect for us." My dick starts to harden inside of her again and she starts to rock on me.

Gripping her face, I run my fingers through her hair and bring her mouth down to mine. "You're fuckin' perfect."

"I love you Stav." She whispers against my lips.

"I love you, too, baby."

I take my time ravaging her body. Every kiss is slow and meaningful. I spend my time making sure that I run my mouth over every inch of her perfect skin. She sucks on my earlobe and I thrust my hips up into her. Her pussy grips me harder than anyone I've ever fucked, and I can't help but slowly grind her down on me.

Her mouth forms an O and she lets her head fall backwards. She slowly rides me and I can't help but feel like one lucky son of a bitch. I run my hands up her body, grab her tits, and give them a good squeeze. She moans out my name as I continue to thrust into her. Sitting up, I pick her up, and get off the couch. Walking us over to the wall, she wraps her legs around my waist, and I push her up against the wall and wrap my hand around her neck and put some pressure on it.

"Oh God." Her breathy moan fills my living room and I fuck her harder. Each thrust is deep and rough. In no time, I have her calling out my name loudly. "Fuck me harder." She gasps. Sliding my other hand down her back, I press her into the back of the couch and gather some of her wetness before starting to work my index finger into her ass.

Every thrust is in sync, and I can feel her body tightening around me. She loves when I fuck her in both her pussy and her ass. She takes everything I give her and always is begging me for more. She is fucking perfect for me, every fucking inch of her beautiful body and mind. Her fingers run along my shoulders and then move to my back. Her nails dig into my skin and I can feel them cutting through. The pain brings me right over the edge, and I feel her pussy clench as she comes with me.

Walking us towards my bedroom, I take my time

kissing her soft, creamy skin. "God, I could get lost in your body all fucking day and night, and still not be satisfied." She giggles and presses a kiss to my lips before I lay her back on the bed. Pulling out of her, I make my way into the bathroom and take a piss before I join her in the bed where she is still sprawled out naked.

Getting involved with her was never my plan. I tried to fight it for so long, but she wore down my defenses. I knew the type of man I was, and I knew I didn't want to corrupt her perfect life. She never wanted for anything and she came from parents who loved her.

Thinking back, I still remember the day that she brought me home with her, and the conversation that followed. Her father gave me a dirty look and refused to even shake my hand. He hated me instantly and part of me thinks that's what she liked so much about me.

She never brought it up, and I never asked. Her mother was different though. She judged me, but she also wanted her daughter happy. The more I came around, the easier it was to deal with her, but I know that she still didn't think I was the man for her daughter. When her father forbade her from seeing me, she cut all ties with them.

She walked out of their lives all because of me. I hated knowing I was the reason for it, but she told me, "I would do anything for you Stavros. I love you. If they can't understand that, then I don't need them in my life."

I had to try and get her to see that I didn't want her to do that. I wanted her to always have her family.

"Baby, they are still your family. You'll always need them." She shakes her head at me and I frown. "What if this shit between us doesn't work out?" She frowns this time and straddles my lap again.

"Are you trying to tell me something?" her voice breaks and I instantly feel bad.

"No, but I want you to always have options just in case."

We didn't talk about it much after that and I wish I would have pushed the issue more, but I just let it go. I wanted her to be happy, and with me she was, well that is until she got kidnapped.

I hear faint crying, but I can't force my eyes to open again. "You love a fucking monster. Do you know what he did to his mother's boyfriend? Do you even care what he did last time he saved you, princess?" Flint's voice rings out in the quiet room.

"I don't care! He loves me. And that's more than

a lot of people have." She sobs. Her shrieks fill the room and I'm glad I can't see them right now. "Just kill me now. I will never do anything you tell me. I don't care if you threaten to kill everyone I know. He's the only one that matters." Her voice is stronger than before. I love knowing that she's strong. She needs to be if she wants to make it out of here alive.

A hand grips my hair and I feel a knife at my throat. Her gasp is loud and I know that I'm a goner after this. There is no way I'll survive once that knife slits my throat. I feel the knife dig into my skin and the blood starts to drip down, and onto my bare chest.

"This bastard is really all that important to you? You're no better than he is if you aren't bothered by the shit he's done to insure that you were never touched by another man." Flint spits at her.

She doesn't back down and yells right back at him. "At least I know that he would give his life for me. No one has ever cared enough to even think about murdering someone to protect me. Stavros would. He did! I even got to beat the fuck out of your little whore Delilah after she fucked up your plan. How does it feel that she didn't even obey you because she wanted Stavros more? Her loyalty to getting him in bed won, and you were left with nothing!"

"She was a lost cause, and once I kill this bastard, you won't have a choice but to be mine. I hope you like it rough, bitch." He barks out with a laugh.

The harder he presses the blade into me, the more blood covers my skin. The door slams open and I hear shouting, and, maybe fighting, but he pushes the knife down harder and cuts deeper into the side of my neck before it's gone, and I go unconscious.

A slap to my face brings me around slightly, but I can't make anything out. No noise, no light, nothing. Everything is dark and my body feels weightless. My cloudy head can't make sense of what's happening.

Chapter Twenty

Hushed whispers fill my ears as I slowly come to. When I open my eyes, everything looks blurry, and I'm having trouble adjusting to the harsh lighting in the room. "Lights." I whisper hoarsely.

Someone moves, and the room is basked in darkness. "Prez." Someone says from beside me and when I try to open my eyes again, I see Romeo sitting on my right side. Looking from face to face, I feel my pulse quicken, but when I don't see her face, I blow out a harsh breath and close my eyes again.

I promised her she would be free when everything was dealt with, and she ran. A small hand lands on mine and I look over to see Trix's tear streaked face. "I'm so glad you're awake." She whispers. She squeezes my hand and I ask her the silent question. She shakes her head no and I lay back against the pillows and close my eyes.

I wanted her to be here. I know it's asking a lot, but I needed to see with my own two eyes that she's alive.

I look around at the rest of my men standing in the room. "Good to see you awake, Prez." Romeo says finally. My eyes land on my brother and I see him looking over my face.

"Is she okay?" I rasp out.

My brother nods his head and clears his throat. "I took her to a safe house. She's shaken up and…" he trails off and I give him a look. He slightly shakes his head, and I drop it.

A few of the others look uncomfortable with the conversation, so I change the subject. "How did you find us?" I ask.

"Nikolai called in a few favors and we had enough fire power and men to bust down the fuckin' doors. We took them all out, and you're fuckin' lucky to be alive. If he would have cut half an inch to the right, he would have severed your artery." Silence fills the room and I see that somber looks on all of their faces.

"Can you guys give us a few." Romeo states, standing up. Everyone takes their time getting up and making their way outside, saying their goodbyes as they walk out. Once everyone is gone, Nikolai and

Romeo both take the seats next to the bed.

"She's in a bad mental state. She watched as that bastard slit your throat. He forced her to stab you, and we don't know how much damage he did to her yet." Romeo says lightly. He doesn't sound like his normal self, and that worries me.

"Can I see her?" I croak out. Every muscle in my body is screaming out in pain as I try to move. Nikolai puts his hand on my shoulder, and gently pushes me back against the bed.

"She doesn't want to see you." Niko states with a firm tone. My eyes shoot to his and then go back to Romeo.

"I'm sorry, brother. She said she wants to be alone. You both just went through a lot. Give her time. She thought you were dead." Instead of saying anything, I just close my eyes.

"Can you give her a message for me?" Niko nods his head and pulls out his phone. He pulls up something on the screen and then hands it over to me.

"It's the prepay I gave her while I work on getting her settled somewhere else." I nod my head at his statement and start to type out a message to her.

Harlyn just know that I will always go to the ends of the earth for you. You're the color in my cloudy life. Thank you for giving me some of your

color. You have no idea what you do for me. I love you and thank you for fighting for me.

I hand the phone back over to Nikolai after I send the message. He doesn't say anything else, and I watch as they both get up and walk out of the hospital room.

I end up spending two painfully shitty weeks in this fuckin' place. My brothers come and go, and I'm rarely alone. It's comforting and suffocating all at the same time. The only person I want to show her face still hasn't come to see me. My wounds and bruises are starting to heal, but they don't erase what happened to us.

When they move me to my house, I look around my bedroom, and can't help but hate the fucking place. The last time I was here was when I had Harlyn in my arms as I fucked her. Closing my eyes, I fight back the memories and put the pillow over my face to all but fuckin yell.

Those fuckers thought that I'd do better here, but they have no fucking clue the memories this place causes. I never want to step foot in this place again, but right now I don't have a choice. I have a broken leg, and I can barely get around due to my injuries.

When Nikolai comes walking in with a bottle of Johnny, I practically salivate. I haven't had a drink in, who the fuck knows, and right now, I would rather drown myself in that bottle than feel the pain in my chest.

"You want it?" He asks. I try to reach out and grab it, but he pulls the bottle back and taunts me with it for a second, like a shitty little brother would do.

"Fuck yes. You know I do, or you wouldn't have brought it. Now hand it the fuck over, asshole." I demand. He finally gives it to me and I unscrew the cap and take a long pull. The liquid burns as it goes down and it takes my mind off of all things Harlyn.

"She asked about you." His words cut deeper than the knife that was fuckin' jammed into my stomach by Flint.

"What did she say?" I mumble. He tosses a card at me and I pick it up off the bed and look at it. Her hand writing is flawless, and the urge to read it takes over everything else.

"Find out for yourself. I'll leave you to it. Just don't drink yourself into a stooper. I have a few things I need to do before I get her shit settled. Uncle Viktor wants to talk to you when you're healed, too." I look up at him and he shrugs. "Don't ask me. I didn't tell him shit, just that I was helping you." I watch him tap the wall with his palm before he makes his way out of the room, and the front door opens and closes.

Looking back down at the card, I flip it over and start to read the writing on the back.

Stavros,

There are so many things I want to say to you right now, but I don't even know where to begin. I'm sure you hate me right now for not being there for you, but I can't. I feel like I don't even know the person that I've become, and I hate myself for it. Just please know that I love you so much and watching them do those things to you… I don't even know how I feel about it.

I thought that you were dead as I watched the blood start to pour from your neck. You got cold and pale. I did everything I could to put pressure on it, but you were losing too much blood. I never wanted to stab you or get that asshole's name tattooed on me, but I did it to save you. I would rather endure pain than know that you weren't walking this earth.

I know you'll continue to protect me and watch over me and I'm thankful for that. I love you more than you'll ever know and I wish I could show you. I wish that I could be there with you right now. Don't forget me and all the love we made. You are worth fighting for Stav, and I wish I had the courage to keep fighting for you.

If you fly, I fly.

I'll love you for forever and a day.

XOXO, Harlyn

I set the card down on the bed next to me and for the first time in forever, I feel a tear slide down my cheek. I don't remember the last time I ever let an emotion affect me this way unless it was lust, anger, or love. Love and lust are the only two things that I ever felt with Harlyn, and right now she's bringing out a new emotion in me. Heartbreak.

Laying back against the pillows, I close my eyes and try to push out all emotion from my head. I don't want to think about anything that has to do with her. I just want to get through this shit and heal so I can get back on my feet, and ride my bike. Fuck, did they ever find my bike?

Grabbing my phone, I wipe my cheeks and dial Romeo's number. When he finally answers, I don't give him a chance to say much. "Did you guys find my bike?" I hear his chuckle across the line, and I want to punch the fucker.

"I'm glad your head is fucking back on straight." He yells something out to someone else and then gets back on the phone. "You can't even ride, why do you care?"

"Because that's one of the only fuckin' things I have left. I need to know that my girl is still up and running for when I'm ready to ride again." He laughs again and I wish I could reach through the fucking phone and deck the bastard.

"Yeah we got your bike. There was some damage, but nothing you can't fix."

"Good. As soon as I can get out of this fuckin' bed, I'm getting her fixed back up and riding. Sitting on my ass is fucking drive me mad." Little does he know that's not the only thing I'll be doing once I can move. I'll be getting an address out of Nikolai and driving by her place to make sure she's okay before I can put her out of my mind completely. Who am I kidding, I can't put her out of my mind.

"You need to heal before you do any of that shit." He grunts out.

"Yeah says the fucker who isn't fucking bed ridden. I want to get the fuck out of here. You know I haven't been here since Harlyn was with me and I can't be here any longer." He grunts out some answer that I don't understand, and I'm itching to get up.

Pushing my body to the edge of the bed, I slip off of it, and swear under my breath. "I'll get a couple of the prospects to come pick you up. Just don't do anything you shouldn't. Stay off your damn leg or you'll never heal right."

"Yes, mother." I snicker. He hangs up and I toss my phone on the bed and make my way to the bathroom to take a piss. By the time the fuckers finally show up to take me to the clubhouse, I'm three sheets to the wind, and all I want to do is fuckin' pass the fuck out in my bed at the clubhouse.

When we finally get there, I make my way to my room and collapse onto my bed, which causes my whole body to feel like I got hit by a mac truck. Burying my face into my pillows, I get a whiff of her perfume and I have to close my eyes. Everything I've ever felt for her floods my mind. I want to open my eyes and have her laying in my arms again like she was only a few weeks ago.

When my eyes open, I don't see anything but the white wall across from me, and it floods my body with anger. I let her get hurt again and now she wants nothing to do with me. I'll never be good enough for her and the sooner I realize this, the less likely I'll fuckin' hurt.

A painful ache takes over my chest and I have to squeeze my eyes closed, as the last moments of Harlyn and I together flood my mind. Walking away from her was a mistake. I should have fought for her. I shouldn't have left her alone in my room.

"Fuck!" I roar. I take the Johnny off my nightstand, chuck the fuckin' bottle at the wall, and watch as it shatters. The liquor spills on the carpet and the glass rains down next to the wall.

Grabbing the nightstand next, I pick it up and throw it against the wall, too. I watch as the wood splinters and crashes to the ground. The monster inside of me wants to go and find her and bring her back here, but the voice in my head is winning out. She deserves better than me. Better than this monster inside of me that forces me to take things from one extreme to the next.

Sinking to the ground by the door, I put my head in my hands and hear boots running down the hallway. When my door opens, Dex and Romeo both look at the mess that I've made, and give me a sad expression.

I don't want their pitty, all I want is to get rid of the pain that is suffocating me right now. I want to get over her, but I know that it'll never happen. She fuckin' owns me mind, body, and god damn soul. No woman will ever take her damn place, and my chest hurts just thinking about it.

"You good?" Dex finally asks.

I shake my head no and look over to the wall. I try to stand up, but I end up losing my balance and falling back into the wall. They step forward to help me, but I push them both away. "Every fuckin' thing reminds me of her. My fuckin' bed smells just like her, and I just want to get away from it all. She doesn't want me, fine. I'll fuckin' deal somehow. Just don't fuckin' feel sorry for me. I made my bed and I'll lie in it for once." I stand up, hobble past them both, and make my way into my office. When I slam my door shut, I picture the day she came back and I fucked her against my desk. Putting my arms on the desk, I get pissed and knock every fuckin' thing off of it. Glass breaks, and papers scatter all over the floor.

She's fucking with my head and I wish it would stop, but I'm a prisoner in my own damn head. She fuckin' owns me and doesn't even fucking care.

Hobbling over to the couch, I lay down and shut my eyes. I have to drown everything out somehow, now if I can only figure out how.

chapter Twenty-One

Three years. Two months. Three days. Sixteen hours.

That's how long I've been waiting for Harlyn to come back to me since everything that went down with the Fighting Rebels. She's been keeping a secret from me that she doesn't think I know about, but she's wrong. When Nikolai called to tell me that she was finally going to come see me, I was fuckin' jumping at the bit.

I can't wait for her to finally tell me the goddamn truth. I deserve to fucking know and if she doesn't tell me soon, I'll make sure she knows that I know, and that I'm not letting her leave again.

I've been watching her from a distance, and this time I haven't tried to get in between her and the life she has right now. I forced my brother to give me her location when I finally healed completely, and I've continued to watch her.

I watch as Niko's car pulls in on the security camera and I see her get out. She looks fucking better than I remember, and I can see her new curves from here. Niko opens the back door and I see a little boy get out of the car. I feel like I've got the fuckin' wind knocked out of me. Niko picks him up, and I watch as Harlyn walks around the car to my brother. He says something to her and she looks up at the camera. She gives me a dirty look and I can't wait for her to get her ass inside. Making my way from my office, I mosey towards the bar and I wait for them.

When the doors open, I see a few people's mouth drop open. They get a look at Harlyn and the little boy that my brother is holding before they look over at me. Everyone here knows what went down three years ago, but no one mentions it.

Trix gives me information when I ask her for it, but I can tell that it bugs her when I want her to spy on her friend for me, so I didn't ask her a lot. She gave me enough to know that she wasn't sleeping with anyone else, and that she missed me. She didn't say anything more than that, but I wasn't really asking her to give me all the details of her life - I just wanted the important parts.

"Stavros." Harlyn all but sneers at me. I know

she's pissed that she's here, but I'm not the one who forced her this time. She came all on her own.

I make my way over to her and wrap my arms around her, pulling her body into mine. I press my mouth to hers, and kiss her roughly. She holds her body tensely, but then gives into me, and kisses me back. "Mommy." A little voice whispers. He looks over at me, and I release her. She wipes her mouth and I can't help but grin at her.

She takes the boy from my brother, and he walks towards the bartender and asks for a drink. "Ruslan, remember when I told you that you were going to meet someone really important?" He nods his head and points at me. She gives him a small smile and nods her head. "This baby, is your daddy." He looks between me and his mother and his eyes keep bouncing back and forth between us.

"Ruslan." The name feels strange on my tongue, but I reach out to him, and he hesitantly reaches out to me. I take him into my arms, and for the first time since she left, I feel at peace.

Wrapping my arm around her neck, I pull her to my body and whisper in her ear, "you're not leaving again."

When she looks up at me, I can see the ghost of a smile cross over her lips. "I'm tired of running from you. I tried to be with someone else and it never felt right. You're it for me Stav." I lean down, press my mouth down on hers, and I kiss her deeply.

Ruslan starts to giggle and says, "gross!"

I release her and she starts to tickle him. "Mommy!" He shrieks. I grab her hand and lead her towards my room.

I know I shouldn't forgive her for not telling me about my son, but I don't want to waste any more time than we already have. I want to have a life with my son and her. Who the fuck knows when the next war, or worse, is going to come at us, at least I know I'll have time with them both. We can be a family.

Shutting them both in my room, Harlyn looks around and notices a few changes from before. We revamped the rooms last year, and got all new furniture. We even had the prospects do some painting.

"What happened to the old stuff?" She asks looking around.

"Well when I got back from the hospital, I may have had some trouble with my anger." I set Ruslan on the bed and he rolls over onto his back and then moves towards the top of the pillows. She raises an eyebrow at me, and I shrug. "I knew you weren't coming back. So my anger got the best of me."

She closes the distance between us and wraps her arms around my waist. "The letter?" She asks quietly. I nod my head and press my forehead to hers.

"It tore me in fuckin' two. I couldn't fuckin' think straight, and when I finally got them to bring me back here because I couldn't sit in the house I bought for you, I flipped. Ended up breaking some furniture and a bottle of Johnny on the wall." Her eyes widen and she looks up at me.

"Stav." She whispers. Her hand cups my face, and I wish I had her with me all this time. It would have saved me a lot of broken furniture, bones, and bottles.

"I want you both to come home with me. I want us to be a family. Me, you and Ruslan." She gives me a smile and stands on her tippy toes to kiss me.

"Home?" she has a mischievous smile on her face and I can't help but lean down to kiss her again.

"Yeah, home. Where your sexy ass should have been years ago. I hate that I've missed out on so much of his life."

She frowns and looks over at him as he closes his eyes on my bed. He's curled up just like Harlyn used to do when I'd have to go on a run. She would lay herself in the middle of my bed, and fall asleep. When I'd get home, she'd still be in the same spot I left her.

"I know you've had Trix and Nikolai getting you information all these years. You've known all this time about him. Why didn't you show up at my doorstep demanding to see your son?" I sit down on the edge of the bed and pull her into my lap.

"Because if I would have dragged your ass back here again, I wouldn't have gotten my girl back, you'd be pissed off at me like last time. Look how well that went last time. You came back kicking, screaming, and hating me. I couldn't do it again. I wanted you to choose me. I wanted you to choose having a family with me."

She smiles and puts her head in the crook of my neck. "Stav, I always wanted a family with you. You're the only one I would ever want to be the father of my child. You weren't in a good place to be a father, and I knew that. As much as it hurt to push you away, I knew I had to, for his sake. I don't always know what is running through your head, and I'm terrified that if he did something wrong you might snap. I couldn't take the chance."

Running my fingers through her hair, I push it out of her face and crane my neck to look at her face. "I would never hurt him, or you." My voice is soft and I see her watching me.

"You always said that to me, but remember I had the bruises to prove otherwise." I close my eyes and put my cheek on her head. Blowing out a breath, I think back to the night she's taking about.

I felt like shit when I left the bruises on her and I hope like hell I never do it again. But then again I can't control it. I've learned to control it a little since she left, but I don't know how much power I have yet. Nikolai has been working with me since he knew how important it was for me to get her back one day, especially since she was pregnant with my kid.

"Harlyn…" I start, but I can't find the words I want to say to her. She has to know that I never meant to leave a bruise on her body. The only mark I ever wanted to leave on her was my name, my club name, my handprint on her ass cheek, and the hickies I used to leave on her neck.

"Stav I know you didn't mean to, but he won't understand. I need you to always be aware of your actions, and to not let whatever it is inside of you take over in front of him. He's a child, and won't understand." I nod my head because I don't even know what to say to her. I want to be the best man I can be for them both, but I'm not sure I always can be.

"I'll always do my best to protect you both and I promise if I'm like that again I won't come home. I'll go to the clubhouse instead." She cups my cheek, and forces me to look into her eyes.

"I love you Stavros. I've loved you since the first time I saw you in this place, and I'll love you until I take my last breath." Pressing my mouth against hers, I kiss her deeply. Her hand slides down my cheek to my neck and she runs her fingers over the scar that now graces my neck.

She follows the length of the scar with her finger and as much as I want to pull away, I don't. I want her to know the damage that bastard Flint did to me, and I just hope that she accepts it. I have a shit ton of new scars that mark my skin, but I wouldn't change any of it. I went to the edges of hell to make sure she was protected, and I would do it again if I had the choice. Her life has always been more important than mine, and if I didn't live through all the torture, we wouldn't be right here right now, and we wouldn't have a beautiful son.

"Did he hurt you?" my voice isn't much more than a whisper, but I need to know. Nikolai never told me what exactly happened to her when she wasn't in the room with me. I watch her expression as she thinks about that time, and her eyes darken before they look back at me.

"He tried. He pushed me on a bed, and tried to pull my jeans off of me, but I fought back as much as I could until I kneed him directly in the dick. He fell to the ground and bitched and moaned for a while before they brought me back into the room with you. Someone shot me up with some drug, and they pushed me against the wall where I had to sit and watch them torture you some more. It was the worst time of my life." A tear falls down her cheek. Using my thumb, I wipe it up and kiss her cheek.

"I can't believe what you had to endure. You went through so much, and there wasn't anything I could do to save you." I grab her hand in mine and I run my fingers over the spot that used to have my name written in ink. She looks down at it too, and I see the frown on her face.

Flint.

The bulky letters are starting to fade a little, but you can still read his name plain as day. "You never got it covered?" I ask. My fingers gently run over it again, and I wait for her answer.

"I thought about it so many times, but could never do it." I look at her and I can't get a read on her. Before I can say something to piss her off, she continues. "I didn't want to forget what happened to us, but I also wanted to wait to talk to you before I did anything. I know you are probably pissed that I still have his name on my skin, but it doesn't mean anything to me. The only thing that I've cared about the last three years was that little boy right there, and figuring out a way to be able to get through what we went through. I watched you die. I felt your last breath, and right then and there, I wanted to die too." A sob comes from her mouth. She looks over at Ruslan before she looks back at me.

"I'm sorry baby." I murmur kissing the top of her head. She curls her body into mine and I hold her closer to me. Three years of not having Harlyn by my side has sucked, and I'm definitely not a saint, but I know deep down that she is the only one that will ever hold my heart.

"I love you so much Stav. It destroyed me. All I could think of was your blood coating my hands. For months, I had dreams of you dead. I had dreams of that asshole Flint standing over your body with your knife dangling in his fingers. I barely slept, and could barely eat. The doctors where worried about me and Ruslan because I was so skinny and tired all the time. Finally Nikolai told me that I was slowly killing myself and our baby." A tear slips down her face. I reach up and wipe it off of her cheek.

It fuckin' kills that I'm the reason behind her tears again. I never wanted for us to be like this. I want us to be a family. I will spend the rest of my life making up for all the shit I've put her through.

Chapter Twenty-Two

After talking for a few more hours with Harlyn, I finally get her and Ruslan home. I spent the last few weeks buying stuff for him, just hoping that she would finally bring him home, where they both belonged. Once I carry him into the house, I hear my phone go off.

Harlyn puts her hand in my pants and grabs my phone, pulling it out, and looking at the screen, she wrinkles her nose and dangles the phone in front of me. "Looks like one of your whores wants a good time from you." Grabbing the phone from her, I silence the call and grab the back of her neck, pulling her to me.

"I only want you." I whisper before I press my mouth over hers, silencing her from saying anything else. She sighs into my kiss, and kisses me back. When she finally pulls away, I carry Ruslan into his room, and set him on his bed that I put together the other night.

"Wow." She breathes when she takes the room in. "You did all this?" I tuck Ruslan in and walk over to where she's standing by the door.

"Yeah. I was hoping that you'd come back. When Niko said you were ready to talk, I prayed that you'd stay with me. I wanted to make sure everything was perfect for both of you." Wrapping a hand around her neck, I walk her backwards out of the room and push her up against the wall outside of his bedroom.

"Stav." She whimpers. She doesn't get a chance to stop me before I pick her up and carry her into our room. The same room I spent so many days and nights worshiping her perfect fucking body. Kissing my way down her neck, I pay special attention to the spot under her ear that drives her insane. Laying her on the bed, I grab her jeans and start to undo them. Her eyes heat up, and she watches me intently.

As I slide them down her tone thighs, I place open mouthed kisses all over her flawless skin. Tossing them on the floor behind me, I make my way back up and spread her legs. My tongue slides between her folds a few times before I make my way back up her body. My fingers slide under her shirt and I start to push it up her body.

"No panties?" I murmur as I kiss her skin. She

starts to squirm under me as I slide her shirt up and over her head. She leans forward and presses her lips against mine.

"Not a huge fan of them." She moans. My fingers slide between her folds and my index finger circles her clit. Grinning against her throat, I press a quick kiss to her skin before pulling away completely. She groans, and I get off the bed. Her naked body is spread across the covers that she picked out all those years ago.

"Stavros." She runs her fingers down her body and I have to bite my cheek to keep from moving over to her. Her eyes roam down my body and stop on my dick trying to break free from the constriction of my jeans. When I don't give her what she wants, she gets to her knees, and pulls me closer to her by the waist of my jeans.

Her hands slip inside, and she brushes her fingers over my dick. He jumps in anticipation and I don't know how much longer I can wait for her. She starts to undo my jeans and pushes them down my thighs. As she comes back up, I watch as her tongue brushes over my tip before she kisses her way up my body, pulling my shirt off as she goes. She's doing the same things I was doing to her.

Once she has my clothes off, she grabs my shoulder, and pushes me back onto the bed. She straddles my lap and lines herself up with my dick. As she slowly sinks down on me, I lean up on my elbows, and watch her expression as I stretch her pussy. Her mouth opens and her head falls back. Thrusting up into her quickly, I hear her moan. Sitting up, I grab her hips and start to move her slowly up and down my length.

Our eyes lock on each other and I get taken right back to the first time. Her long hair tossed over her shoulder. Her eyes watch every move I make. Leaning forward, I capture her mouth with mine, and she starts to move faster. Her tits are fuller than before. I grab them and give them a squeeze. She moans, and grabs the back of my neck to steady herself. "Stav." She moans louder. "I'm going to come." Her pants are coming out quicker and I'm about to come, too. It's been far too long since I've had her sweet pussy wrapped around me.

She moves her hips in a circle and I reach down to rub her clit. Her fingers dig into my neck and she starts to yell out my name, but I cover her mouth with mine as she rides out her orgasm. Her tits press against my chest and her nails dig deeper into my skin causing me to come right behind her. Before we can even come down from our orgasms I hear Ruslan's small voice from the door way.

Harlyn buries her face into my neck and I can feel her body racking with silent laughter. "Momma?" When she can finally keep a straight face, she turns her head to face our son.

"Yeah baby?" My hand is still on her ass and I try

not to move much. This kid will get an eyeful if I do.

"I baf reem." I lean her back and grab my shirt of the ground so she can pull it on. Once she has it on, she slowly moves up and off of me, and I groan as I slide out of her. She turns so I'm still covered she hands me my jeans before going over to Ruslan.

I pull on my jeans as she pulls him into her chest. Watching her, I can't believe how fuckin' lucky I am. "What was your dream about?" she asks him softly.

"Hurring momma." He starts to cry and she wraps him up in her arms and comes walking back over to the bed with him. I scoot back against the pillows and she hands him over to me. Sitting him in between us, I wait for Harlyn to join us under the covers.

"Someone hurt momma in your dream?" I ask softly. He looks up at me with sad eyes and nods his head. He curls up into my side and when I look up at Harlyn, I see a sad smile on her face. When Ruslan looks back up at me, I give him and Harlyn both a promise. "I'll never let anyone hurt you, or momma."

He seems happy with that answer, so he curls up into my side and closes his eyes. Harlyn runs her fingers through his dirty blonde hair and then looks back up at me. "Thank you Stav." She whispers. I watch her scoot closer to us both, and she lays down on her side to face me.

Reaching over to her, I run my fingers over her

face and stop at her lips. "You know I'll always protect you. I may have failed at it last time, but this time I won't."

"You never failed at it. You've always protected me. You almost died to save my life." I turn to look up at the ceiling for a second before I look back at her.

"I didn't protect you. You should have never seen anything that happened in that place. You watched me kill a man in there. I—" she cuts me off before I can keep going.

"You did what you had to. You saved me. Who knows what that man would have done to me if you hadn't killed him. You saved me, Stavros." I shake my head no, but she reaches over and grabs my face, forcing me to look at her.

"Don't act like this was your fault. I love you, and that is never going to change. You did what you had to in order to protect me, and for that I'm grateful. If you didn't, we wouldn't have this little boy." She runs her fingers through his hair again before she looks back at me.

"Yeah, but it didn't stop you from leaving me again." The words come out harsher than I expected them to, but I can't take them back now even if I tried. She looks hurt, but she doesn't let that hold her back any. Her feisty personality comes shining through.

"I left because I had to. Watching you die, or,

almost die, as your brother put it, was the hardest thing I've ever had to do. I could have watched you kill a hundred more people and stayed, but watching as the life drained out of you wasn't something I could live with." She whisper yells at me. She's trying not to wake Ruslan and every time she looks down, I can see a little of her mask slip.

"I didn't even know you had a brother until a few days before everything happened, and the first time I ever met him was the day he came and saved us." A tear slips down her cheek and I want to reach out and wipe it from her face, but I stay rooted to my spot on the bed. "How could you not even care enough to call him, or your mother? I don't get it." She shakes her head this time and leans over to kiss Ruslan before slipping out of the bed.

Getting up, I follow after her as she makes her way into the kitchen. I watch her put both hands on the counter before she turns around to face me. "Your brother has been the only man in Ruslan's life since he was born, and even though I know that it's my fault, I can't help but think that you and Nikolai are so damn similar. He was amazing with Rus as a baby, and I hate myself for taking that away from you. I'm a terrible person for not giving you the chance to be there for our son. I can't—"

Putting my finger to her lips, I force her to stop talking. Her eyes darken and I can tell she's pissed that I forced her to be quiet. "Stop." I close the distance between us, and trap her against the counter. Her green eyes are bright with anger and I know that she isn't going to let me keep her where I have her for long.

"I get why you left. I don't blame you for it. Shit, I might have even sent you away from me after I got out of the hospital if you'd stayed. Everything I did and everything anyone said set me off. I was my own worst fuckin' enemy. You didn't need me bringing you down, and I sure as hell didn't want to do anything to hurt you. I have already hurt you enough. All I want to do was love you and I always make a mess of things." I press my forehead to hers for a second before I continue.

"You leaving again was both a blessing, and a curse, all at the same damn time. I needed you to walk away. It fuckin' killed me inside to know that you would live without me again, but I needed it. I wouldn't have been the man you needed. Nikolai kept me at a distance from you for a reason, and I can't thank him enough. Sure, I didn't get to be part of either of yours or Ruslan's life, but I was able to get my shit together enough to provide a future for both of you." A tear slides down her cheek and this time I wipe it off.

Her arms go around my waist and she pulls me closer to her body. Cupping her cheek, I pull her in for a kiss. She melts into my body and I pick her up to sit onto the counter. She wraps her legs around my waist and I can feel her wet heat through my jeans.

"You slept with other women." Her voice is

barely a whisper, and I hate that I'm about to break her heart again.

"Harlyn…" I start, but I can't find the words. She looks towards the ground and I run my fingers along her cheek.

"No, don't. I don't want to know what you were doing with the whores while I was pregnant, giving birth, and raising our son." Closing my eyes, I pull away from her. The bitterness we both carry doesn't help us at all. I want to start clean with her, but I know that it's never going to happen.

"I'm sorry I continue to hurt you. Maybe you were right before. All we do is hurt each other. I don't want Ruslan to see that. I'll leave you guys the house and we can work something out with raising him." I turn to walk away and she doesn't stop me.

Walking into the master bedroom, I grab the only remaining clothes I left here and throw them into my bag. I'll figure out a way to be in his life even if I can't be in hers. Placing a kiss on his forehead, I watch him for a second before I make my way out of the room and past Harlyn who is still sitting in the kitchen.

"Stav." She whispers. I look over at her and she has tears running down her face. She slides off the counter and comes over to me. Seeing the pain on her face, I can't stay here any longer. Her hands land on my stomach, and as much as I want to grab her and pull her to me, I don't. I don't do anything but watch her.

"Please don't leave us. He needs you. I need you." Tears fall faster down her face.

"Harlyn," I start. The heartbreak written all over her face kills me, and I want to make it go away, but I can't. It's never going to leave. I'll always hurt her. She deserves a better man than I'll ever be for her. All I am is a biker with a fuckin' temper, and that doesn't mix with kids. Ruslan doesn't deserve to live in my shadow, and at least with Nikolai watching over them I know that they will always be safe.

"I'll always love you babe. But you'll never be completely happy with me if you're always thinking I'm fucking all the club whores." Her expression falls and I know that I need to just walk away now.

Chapter Twenty-Three

Pulling into the clubhouse parking lot, I see Romeo standing by the doors waiting for me. "Never thought I'd see the day," he says with a frown on his face.

"See the day where I felt like gutting you?" I mutter. He snorts at my answer before he slaps me on the back and walks with me inside the clubhouse.

"No, the day you came back here instead of being at home with Harlyn and your son." I shake my head and walk towards the bar without even bothering to comment on his statement. It's just going to piss me off, and I'm trying to be good, even though shit is all fucked up again.

"Prospect, get me a beer." I shout out. He comes back with one quickly, and I take a swig before Romeo has the chance to sit down and say anything.

"Why the fuck are you here instead of getting pussy from your girl?" He asks, as he takes a seat on the barstool next to me.

"I walked out, okay? Is that what you fuckin' want to know? She still doesn't fuckin' trust me. She thinks that all I've been doing for the last three years is fucking any bitch with a pulse, and you and I both know that ain't fuckin' true. I've slept with one bitch since she's been gone, and somehow, I'm the fuckin' bad guy." He shakes his head and I chug some of my beer.

"She'll never trust me, so why should I fuckin' try anymore." I put my hand to my head and lean against it. Did I screw this shit up between us? Yeah, probably, but I don't think I am the only one to fuckin' blame. We haven't been together in over three years. She didn't even bother to tell me I had a kid until tonight, and now I'm the fuckin' bad guy. I know she wasn't no fuckin' Virgin Mary while she was with my brother. I watched them for months. I saw the way Nikolai watched her, and I know that there is something going on between them.

Pulling my phone out of my pocket, I dial Nikolai's number and wait for him to answer. I probably shouldn't call him since I'm pissed at him right now, but he was the one who brought them home to me. "Yeah?" He finally answers out of breath on the sixth ring. I hear some bitch moaning in the background, and it makes my chest hurt. That could be Harlyn. Closing my eyes, I try to calm myself down before I say anything I regret to him.

"Stavros what the fuck do you need?" He grits out.

"I need you to watch Harlyn and Ruslan." He grunts something out to the bitch he's fucking and she whines a bit before he gets back on the line.

"Why I thought you were taking that shit over?" He questions like I don't know what happened earlier.

"I ended things with her." I mutter. I hear a string of fucks, shits, and dammits before he says anything to me.

"You're fucking shitting me right?" he barks out in laughter.

"No I'm not. You seem to fuckin' know something I don't, so spill it." I grind out. I'm tired of being the last person to know everything when it comes to Harlyn.

"You are the dumbest son of a bitch I've ever met. You left the fucking mother of your child for some stupid ass fucking reason, huh? What, she call you a fuckin' man whore? Well guess what fucker, you are. She found you in bed with two fuckin' bitches a few months before she gave birth. She tried to play that shit off like she didn't care that you were fuckin' around, but it destroyed her." My whole body goes cold.

"What the fuck are you talking about? I never

had a fucking three some since I've been with her. The last fuckin' time I was part of a three some was when Harlyn wanted to try it with Trix." I try and rack my brain for anything that would bring me back to having a threesome in the last three year,s and my mind draws a blank.

"You mean to tell me the president of an MC doesn't do three somes?" My brother asks with a snotty tone. He's lucky he isn't here right now or I'd punch him.

"I fuckin' swear on my son's life. I haven't fucked two women since Harlyn and Trix." I look over at Romeo and he just shrugs his shoulders.

"Then who the fuck was in your room?"

"No fuckin' clue, but it wasn't me." I state looking around the room. Everyone looks fucking happy getting drunk, but the only thing I can think of is who the fuck set her up to see that?

A hand slides on my shoulder and I feel lips on my neck. "Stavros baby, let's go have some fun." She purrs. When I turn around, I see Diamond, one of our whores standing beside me. I shake her off and go back to listening to Nikolai.

"Well she got a fucking eye full, and swears it was you. Ever since then she hasn't trusted a word you said, and another reason she didn't want you to know about Ruslan. She was trying to protect both herself and him." He whispers something to the bitch in the background, and I can't help but think about Harlyn.

"I only fucked one bitch while she's been gone, and I only fucked her mouth. Well, I take that back, I fucked Harlyn earlier, but she's the first pussy I've had wrapped around my dick since before she was taken by Flint."

"Fuck," he mutters. "I don't need to know this shit. She's like a little fucking sister to me. Have you ever thought to, I don't know, talk to her? You want that shit to work with her, then fucking talk to her. You both are so damn stubborn that I can't talk any damn sense into either of you." He mutters something else, but I don't catch the words this time.

"She's the one that just fuckin' assumes shit." I grate out.

"Did you ever think to try and tell her the damn truth? Or are you too much of a coward?"

"Fuck you, Nikolai." I yell before hanging up on him. Getting off my stool, I make my way to my room alone, and slam the door behind me. Throwing myself on to the bed, I look around the room, and my eye catches the photo that Harlyn forced me to take with her years ago. Getting up, I make my way over to the mirror that she taped it to, and pull it off.

Her plump lips are the first thing I see, and I crave them. I crave the taste of her sweaty skin after I fuck her long and hard. Closing my eyes, I take a minute to think about all the shit we've gone through in the last eight and a half years. We've had some of our best moments together, and now we even have a little boy who is the mirror image of both of us.

A text brings me back from my thoughts and when I see the number that Nikolai gave me for her, I hit the open button and stare at the words.

Harlyn: **Stavros I'm sorry. I don't want to lose you. I was a bitch, and I'm afraid of jumping in head first with you again. My heart can't take any more heartbreak. We both need you in our lives. Please.**

Staring at my phone, I don't even know how to process this shit anymore. I'm tired of being the reason behind her tears, and I don't want to be the reason she's unhappy either.

Me: **You're not a bitch babe. You're protecting yourself and our son. I get it.**

Harlyn: **No! Stav, please. I just want to start over.**

How the hell do we start over? There is no way in hell that we can ever start over. She knows the deep dark secrets I keep inside of me. Raising a son with me isn't something that she should want, and, fuck, she doesn't need me to fuck everything up again.

Instead of writing her back, I shut off the screen

to my phone and set it on the table next to the bed. Stripping down, I get under the covers and try to think about anything but her sweet face. Finally being able to fall asleep a few hours later, I'm just happy to have them both closer to me.

The door clicks shut quietly and I reach for my gun. I watch the shadow come closer to me but before the person can get too close, I point my gun right at the shadow. She gasps, and I put the gun down on the table next to my phone. "What are you doing here?" I ask reaching over to turn on the light.

She walks closer and then crawls into bed with me. "You stopped answering, and I couldn't leave us like that. Stav, I love you too much to let you go. I know my actions over the last four years probably don't make you think that I'm serious this time, but watching you walk out that door earlier was the hardest thing I've ever done." Her sad eyes look up at me, and her cold body touches mine.

"I cried for hours until Nikolai showed up. He told me about your conversation with him, and I finally understand that I'm just over dramatic. I never asked you for the truth, I just assumed that you were doing all those things. He told me that you swore that you weren't the one I walked in on, and I want to believe that. I need to." She looks away almost like she's embarrassed that she admitted that.

"Harlyn..." I start, but I don't know what to even say to her anymore.

"No don't. I know you're going to tell me that we just need to move on, but I don't want to. I know you don't really want to either Stav." She has me there. I never want to let her go, but right now I don't think I have a choice.

"Harlyn we don't work together. We haven't since..." I trail off and she absently rubs her neck. I'm thankful they never fucking hurt her while Flint and his gang of fuck ups had her. The scars of the past still hit me like a ton of bricks though, and I hate knowing that she went through that because of me. I reach out and stop her hand from rubbing the scar on her neck.

"We do work together. I call you a selfish asshole, and you tell me I'm being a pain in the ass. We love each other. Doesn't that count for something?" Closing my eyes, I lay back against the headboard. I can feel her watching me, but I still don't open my eyes.

"You've also told me that I was ruining your life." She frowns at my words, and I can't help but move the hair out of her face. She looks down at my chest and doesn't say anything for a few minutes.

"I was angry. I had just seen Dex kill the guy I was dating because he tried to get in between Dex and I. Your best friend all but dragged me out of my apartment with a dead body on the floor. You can't honestly hold what I said to you after that against me. You took away my choices and I hated you for it, but I know you did it to protect me. You always do what you have to in order to protect me." A tear slips down her cheek and she quickly wipes it from her face. "You even gave me time when I'm sure you didn't want to."

Grabbing the picture that I had earlier, I hand it over to her and I hear her start to cry. Moving down in the bed, I pull her cold body into mine and hold her close to me while she cries. She never lets the photo go, and I know that she misses us, just like I do. The old us was unbreakable until it was shattered on the floor of a warehouse in the middle of fuckin' nowhere.

"The only good decision I've made in the last three years was Ruslan. Having him made me feel like I was finally doing something right. I kept him from you, and that is something I'll have to live with. I've made so many mistakes Stav, but I don't want letting you leave to be one of them. I would do anything to be able to raise our son together as a family." I can feel my body heat at her words and I want to say fuck it and give in, but I don't.

"If we do this, we need to both be all in. No more

going back and forth and walking out when shit gets fuckin' hard. Babe, it will never be easy for us. If you really want to do this, then we play by my rules." Her eyes meet mine and she waits for me to continue. "We go slow. I live here, you and Ruslan stay at the house." Her head drops, and I cup her cheek forcing her to look at me again. "I don't want to keep fucking this shit up. I want us to finally get through all this shit and be together, but the way we've been doing it doesn't work. Let's just give it a go and start over."

"Does that mean I'll finally get a date with you?" her mouth inches closer to mine, and all I can do is stare at her perfect mouth.

"I'll take you wherever you want to go as long as we can start over fresh. No using the past to piss the other off, only focusing on Ruslan and us." I whisper against her lips.

"Okay, I'm in. Does that mean we can't have sex either?" She asks with a raised eyebrow.

"Did you put out the first time we started hanging out?" I grin.

"No, someone wouldn't let me." She pouts. I bite her bottom lip and suck it into my mouth.

"Sorry babe, but I wouldn't want an easy lay as my future wife." Her eyes shoot to mine and she just stares at me in shock.

"Future wife?" She asks hesitantly.

"Yeah, I don't like her having other men's names on her either." She looks down at her wrist and then back up at me.

"That I can definitely take care of." Her grin is wide and I know that someday I will make her my wife.

Chapter Twenty-Four

Two Months Later

The last two months I've spent more time taking Harlyn and Ruslan out on dates. Every day that I get to spend with them is like getting a second chance at life. They make me a better man, and I couldn't thank Harlyn enough for that. Without her showing up at the clubhouse after I walked out, I would have never given us the real shot at this happiness that we both wanted so damn much.

Walking into the clubhouse, I see Romeo and Dex talking at the other end of the bar. When I make my way over to them, they both look up with smiles on their faces. "What are you two doing?" I ask, taking a seat on the barstool.

"You seem different." Dex states. Romeo elbows

him and I can't help but laugh.

"Seriously? That's what you two are talking about in the fuckin' corner?" They both give me a look and I just ignore it.

"So how are things going on the home front? You finally going to move in with them and become a family man?" Dex asks. He motions for a beer and the prospect brings us each one. "And don't fucking act like you and Harlyn aren't fucking still. I ain't blind and you can't hide your white ass behind a wall." They both start to laugh and the doors to the clubhouse open.

"Fuck you. Maybe if you stayed the fuck out of the back you wouldn't have to see my ass." I laugh. I hear something fall to the ground behind us and when I look back, I see Ruslan picking up a box that he must have dropped. Getting off my stool, I walk over to him and look around for Harlyn. "Where is your momma?" I ask, helping him pick up the spilled contents.

Looking at a few of the things, I look up and search for Harlyn, but still don't see her. "Momma me to give you." He hands the box to me, and I pick him up.

I walk him over to the couch and we sit down as he opens the box for me. We start to pull out each item individually, and every time I hear someone coming towards us, I look up hoping that it's Harlyn. She's been moody the last few weeks, and now I know why. "What box for?" Ruslan asks.

He hands me the last item that is a stack of Polaroid pictures. The first one is of Harlyn in a dress that I bought her six years ago. She has a bright smile on her face and I remember why. She had just told me that she wanted to marry me one day. The next picture is of us kissing that she took when I was trying to get her pants off of her a few days later. The third photo is of Ruslan that only looks like it is a few days old. Going to the last photo, I feel my heart start to hammer against my chest.

Getting up, I motion for Romeo to watch Ruslan for a second, and I go outside to find Harlyn. When I finally lay my eyes on her, she has a nervous smile on her face. She's ringing her hands together and I can't imagine why she's hiding out here. She's never been one to stop from telling me what she's feeling or telling me that she's mad, hurt, or anything else.

Walking over to her, I pull her in my arms, and look down at her face. She doesn't say anything at first, but I can tell she's trying to figure out what to say. "The box…" I pause for a second and watch the way she gets nervous. "Are you trying to tell me something?" My lips turn into a grin and she smacks my shoulder.

"Stav." She whispers.

"You either want to tell me that you want to get married or that you're pregnant." Relief floods her features and she looks away for a second before she looks at me again.

"Which one do you want?" her voice is quiet, and almost unsure of what my answer will be. She still has no fuckin' clue how I feel about her.

"Personally, I don't care which I get right now, but at some point I want both." Her eyes widen with my answer and her fingers dig into my sides. "But I've been wondering why you've been so fuckin' bitchy lately, and now I know. Did you really put my brother through this much when you were pregnant with Ruslan?" She slaps my chest, but I pull her closer to me. There is no fuckin' way in hell that I'm letting her leave now.

"No. I don't know why I've been a bitch other than I was scared to tell you. We're supposed to be starting over, not having another baby." I feel her intake of breath, so I lead her over to a bench by the door to the clubhouse. Sitting her down, I kneel down in front of her, and take her face into my hands.

"Harlyn, everything will be fine. Sure we never seem to be doing shit the right way, but these last few months have been amazing. I've gotten to know you better than I ever did before, and I get to be a father to Ruslan." I wipe a stray tear off her face with my thumb, and lean closer to place my lips against hers. "I love you, babe. That will never change. Another kid won't change that. This time I won't have to watch you go through it from afar, I'll get to experience it with you."

She kisses my lips gently. "I'm sorry for being all emotional. These damn hormones are driving me crazy." Brushing a strand of hair out of her face, I give her one more kiss before I stand up, and pull her up too.

"You could be a fucking blubbering mess right now and I'd still think you're the most beautiful woman I'll ever know. You're the mother of my son, and soon to be the mother of my next child. I love you Harlyn. It's never going to change."

She wraps her arms around my neck and hugs me close to her body. "I love you Stav. It's always been you."

Once she wipes her eyes, I grab her hand and lead her back inside. When we walk through the door, Ruslan comes running at us. Picking him up, I look up to see a huge smirk on Romeo and Dex's faces. "Does this mean we get to throw a party, Prez?" Dex asks rubbing his hands together.

"Totally up to her." I say pointing at Harlyn. She looks at me with a questioning expression.

"Oh come on, Harlyn. Let's have a party to celebrate your guy's news." These guys would have a damn party for anything. I used to be like that before I met Harlyn, but the party scene got old when I could spend my nights tangled up in her instead.

"Sure, why not?" She shrugs her shoulder, and before she can say anything else to them, she takes off running towards the bathroom at the end of the bar.

"What's wrong with momma?" Ruslan asks as his eyes follow her to the bathroom.

"She doesn't feel good buddy." I answer, handing him off to Dex so I can go check on her. "I need you to stay with Dex, okay?" He nods his head and I go towards the bathroom she just ran to. Knocking lightly on the door, I push it open and see her hunched over a toilet puking up everything she has in her stomach.

Grabbing a napkin, I wet it, and walk over to her. Placing the napkin on her neck, I hold her hair back. "This is all your fault." She pouts before she finally stands up and flushes the toilet.

"Says the bitch who fuckin' climbs me like a damn tree every time I'm in the same room as her." She frowns and walks over to the sink to wash her mouth out with water.

"You're never touching my pussy again after this baby is born." She groans. I hand her a napkin and raise an eyebrow at her. She really thinks that she's going to keep me from claiming what's mine, she's got another thing coming.

Walking over to her, I wrap my arms around her waist and pull her body into mine. "You and I both know that you won't give up my dick." She pushes my chest and I just smirk at her.

"No, I won't. But you're not the one who has to

push a baby out of your vagina. That shit hurts like a motherfucker." She checks her reflection in the mirror, so I press her hips into the small counter.

"I don't doubt that baby girl, but you and I both know that you'll be begging me for my dick every day up until the day you spit that kid out, and even afterwards." She scoffs at me before pushing past me. She opens the door and makes her way towards were I left Ruslan and Dex.

She takes Ruslan from Dex and gives me the stink eye before walking towards the front door. I follow behind them with a grin on my face, and catch her before she makes it to her car. Even after all this time, she gets an attitude with me when shit doesn't go the way she wants. Not that I'm complaining - I love when she's like this.

I watch as she puts Ruslan in the back seat and straps him into his chair. When she goes to shut the door, I grab it, and move her ass out of the way. Giving Ruslan a kiss on the cheek, I tell him that I love him before I turn my attention back to Harlyn.

Harlyn moves away from me and I shut the door. "Why the pissed off attitude?" I ask, wrapping an arm around her. Her hands go to my stomach and she tries to keep a small distance between us. She doesn't answer me, but she does shrug her shoulders.

"Babe, you know I would do anything for you -

that includes switching places with you right now. But we both know that I would be the worst pregnant person ever." She starts to giggle, and I open the driver's side door to the car I bought her when she came back. Her not having a car was not an option. Apparently she relied on my brother way more than I thought.

"Yeah, you are the worst sick person ever." She's still laughing and I'm just glad to put a smile back on her face. "I love you Stav." She leans forward on her tip toes before pressing a soft kiss to my mouth. "Are you coming over tonight?"

Wrapping my hand in her hair, I pull her head back and force her to look up at me. "Yeah. I'll bring dinner." She grins and nods her head at me before I release her.

"Good, I can be dessert." She gets a devious smirk on her face, and I love the way she thinks.

"Your pussy is my favorite dessert." I nip at her lips and she wraps her arms around my neck. "I love you Har. I'll see you both later." She nods and I help her into the car. I give Ruslan one last wave before she puts the car in reverse and takes off towards the house.

Making my way back inside the clubhouse, I see Dex and Romeo still in the same place I left them. "Trouble in paradise?" Romeo murmurs.

"Naw. Pregnancy hormones apparently. I have a

dinner date with them later and her pussy for dessert."
They both laugh and clap me on the shoulder before
making their way out the door. Instead of hanging
around here, I make my way to my bike to run a few
errands, and grab a few things before I head over to the
house with dinner.

By the time I pull into the driveway of my house,
my saddle bags are full, and I can't wait to get inside.
Collecting the bags, I carry them all to the door at once,
because I hate making more than one trip. I knock on
the door and I hear Ruslan's giggles come from the
other side before the door opens and his little arms
wrap themselves around my legs.

"Daddy!" He squeals. Harlyn giggles as Ruslan
almost takes me out.

"Hey buddy. I got you something." He squeals
again, and this time Harlyn grabs him and pulls him
inside with her.

Once I drop all the bags on the counter and set
the food next to them, I reach into a bag to find the new
toy I bought for Ruslan. Putting it behind my back, I
walk over to them and kneel down in front of him. He
had been going on about this toy for weeks, and Harlyn
kept telling him that she couldn't afford it. That's also
the same day she told me she wanted to get a job, and
I told her no. She pouted like a child for a few hours,
but gave up after I fucked her with my mouth the rest of
the night.

"Your momma sent me out to get something for you." I start. His eyes light up and he starts to bounce around like a little energizer bunny. "But it comes with a stipulation." He gives me a strange look and I keep going. "You're going to have a very important job coming up, and this is because me and your momma know you're going to do an amazing job at it."

"What?" He asks excitedly.

I look up at Harlyn and she kneels down beside me. "You're going to be a big brother." She says with a smile.

"I am?" He asks looking between us. She nods and I see a tear slip from her eyes.

"Yeah buddy. So your momma wanted to celebrate you becoming a big brother because we both know you'll do an amazing job." He nods his head eagerly, and I pull his present out from behind my back and he starts to squeal in excitement.

"You got it! Yas!" He plows Harlyn over, and they both fall to the ground. "Luv yew momma!" He places a kiss on her face and hugs her tightly. Moments like these are what I now live for.

Before, nights with my brothers and Harlyn were all I wanted. But seeing this little boy's eyes light up with love for his mom and me makes everything I've done and gone through worth it all. I will do everything in my power to protect him and his little brother or sister. Harlyn and Ruslan saved me in a lot of ways and I wouldn't trade that in for the world.

The End <3

K. Renee

About the Author

K. Renee is from sunny California. Creative by nature, she decided to put her imagination on paper. During the day, she works in an office; at night, she writes. These stories have been in her head for years and are finally coming out on paper.

http://kreneeauthor.net

https://www.facebook.com/kayreneeauthor

k.renee.author@gmail.com

Tsu: KReneeAuthor

Twitter: k_renee_author

https://www.goodreads.com/user/show/36533772-k-renee

K. Renee

Acknowledgements

First and foremost, I want to thank everyone for buying this book! I never thought I would be releasing one book, let alone writing as many as I have in this short amount of time.

I can't wait for everyone to meet my characters and fall in love with them like I have.

I want to thank my beta readers for giving their honest opinion about the book and my in house beta reader (mom)... You ladies are awesome! Thank you for taking time out of your schedules to beta read for me. I am thrilled that you loved these characters as much as I did.

A big thank you to TCB Editing for doing their editing magic for me. I love getting their feedback on scenes. It truly helps!

To my street team, K's Wayward Ladies... Thank you for all you do! You girls are amazing at pimping my book out to the indie world. Thank you for your support and I can't wait to see what the future brings.

To the readers and fans… I thank each and everyone one of you who come to hang out with me during takeovers, participating in my giveaways! I hope you like this and my future books.

-K